I0591962

ETHAN CROSS AND THE MYSTERE OF THE CORAL SEA

SILENT KEY

R.W. BELL

Author of

TRACE ELEMENT

Table of Contents

"It is a capital mistake to theorize before one has data.
Insensibly one begins to twist facts to suit theories, instead
of theories to suit facts."

- Sherlock Holmes

| Prologue |

The Seed

Mahia Penisula. New Zealand

Albert spoke excitedly to his son as he focused his telescope on the fully fueled rocket.

"Sean, loosen your swivel mounts. It's T-minus 2 minutes!"

"Ok, Papa. I'm going to watch the fairings re-enter. No one ever watches the fairings." Sean released the friction mounts of the English yoke of his new high magnification compound Cassegrain telescope. He trained his optic on the nose cone's aeroshells. Disposable aerodynamic encasements he knew the spacecraft would shed high in the upper atmosphere.

"Ha!" Albert chuckled. "You'll miss the booster reentry helicopter snatch. That's the best part!"

"I've seen it a dozen times, Papa. I'm going to watch the aeroshells burn up this time." Sean focused his instrument across Hawke's Bay at the rocket poised on the launch pad at Ahuriri Point, the southernmost tip of the Mahia Peninsula, on the east coast of New Zealand's North Island.

The native Kiwi father and son pair had watched

nearly all of Rocket Sci's launches this year, an impressive record given the launch site supports up to 120 launches annually. The zealots were proud to tell anyone who would listen that they had observed every one of the one hundred launches sponsored jointly by the N.Z. Space Agency and the Australian Space Agency in the last ten months. Launches like the one ready to ignite in just over 1 minute.

They were set up on their favorite hill, south of the city of Napier, and just outside their hometown of Clifton, well beyond the eight-kilometer radius of the safety exclusion zone from the pad. It was 50 miles across Hawke's Bay, but they would hear the mighty signature of lift-off nonetheless. As always, they would set a timer at lift-off and wait for the low rumble of the blast to reach their vantage point. The sound, traveling unobstructed across the open bay, would get to their ears when the rocket was high in the sky, reminding them of an ignition that occurred minutes before. Albert had told his son that the peninsula's Maori name "Te Māhia" comes from "Te Māhia-mai-tawhiti," which means the sound heard from a distance. Surely, he thought, the native tribes of old referred to the sound of crashing waves, not a rocket's sonic boom.

Sean focused his new telescope onto the pad.

"Papa, I can see the ice on the rocket! Come see." The pair was familiar with the observation of the rocket fuselage frosting over before launch as the moist air condensed and froze on the chilled hull of the rocket now filled with super cooled fuel. Albert peered through his son's new optic, "Yes, I see it. This is a powerful new instrument," he aimed the telescope to the top of the projectile, "and it looks like this one is another twisty-cone." Twisty-cone was their name for the rockets with nose cones having fairings with separation seams that twisted in a spiral from the nose's base to the rocket's apex. The amateur observers likened these rockets to ice cream cones. Albert noted it in their observation journal and remarked, "I would say two-thirds of Rocket-Sci's launches have been twisty cones now. It certainly seems like the majority of them anyway. What do you make of it, Sean? T-minus 30 seconds!" Albert took his position back at his eyepiece.

"I don't know, Papa, but I'm going to keep my eye on those fairings this time," Sean readied himself to pan his telescope skyward to follow the rockets' ascent.

"T-minus five seconds, four, three, start the stopwatch, Sean! Lift-off!" Albert said excitedly.

Sean started the timer and watched the rocket rise slowly at first. It emerged powerfully from the cloud of steam billowing from the pad. Sean knew the steam resulted from millions of gallons of water being pumped to the launch pad in a vain attempt to muffle the roar of the spacecraft as it forcibly clawed its way free from the earth's gravity. At one minute into the launch, Sean observed the familiar pressure wave as the spacecraft pushed through the bow of maximum dynamic pressure.

At 2 minutes 30 seconds, the first stage separated from the upper stage. A few seconds after the first stage shutdown, the second stage's reliable vintage single vacuum-optimized Rutherford engine began to fire, sending its upper stage to orbit. Albert busied himself at the controls of his telescope, followed the first stage as it descended on its way back to its airborne rendezvous; Its propellants exhausted. Its engines extinguished. Albert wanted to witness the first stage deploy parafoils to slow down its descent for protection, allowing it to endure the heat of reentry. He was eager to watch them be plucked out of the sky by a helicopter. It was a recovery maneuver that he had witnessed many times before. He knew it was an operation that allowed the launches from Ahuriri Point to occur at such a high rate. It was not the same spectacle as a propulsive landing on a seaborne autonomous platform used by SpaceX that his friends in America could witness routinely. He knew that the recovery method wasn't suitable for a small launch vehicle like Rocket Sci's. Aero-thermal deceleration, essentially using the atmosphere to slow down the rocket, was the most cost-effective way for his beloved national space agency to maintain the impressive launch cadence they needed to make the economics work. The sequence impressed Albert nonetheless. After the stage reached its maximum velocity, it would coast to an apex and begin its descent. It would hit about Mach 2 on reentry before deploying its pilot chute, then a drogue chute for about a minute to get its speed down, then the main glider chute under which it would cruise along a predictable path until being picked out of the sky by the helicopter. The calculations told him that the spent stage would slow from many times the speed of sound, decelerated to about 10 km per hour in about 70 seconds, and he didn't want to miss it.

Sean kept his powerful instrument trained on the second stage in eager anticipation of the fairing separation. The final section was now high in the upper atmosphere, and the separation would occur in 45 seconds.

Albert spoke an excited reminder to his son without pulling his eye from his reticle. "Get ready with the stopwatch...one minute before the sound wave hits us."

Sean didn't respond to his father. He concentrated intently on the scene unfolding in his aperture. The fairings opened from the craft like a flower awakening to the dawn's first rays of sunshine. The five fairings peeled down and away from the second stage fuselage like a blooming flower. Sean followed the group of spent hardware as they fell together through the thin upper atmosphere toward the surface of the earth. The boy was fixated, eager to see the set of fairings ignite from the atmospheric friction of reentry. The group descended into the thicker lower atmosphere...

"Did you hear me, Sean? It won't be long now before we hear the launch. It's almost T+4minutes."

"Papa, you have to see this." Sean ignored his father's reminder.

"What is it?" There was annoyance in Albert's voice. Albert wanted to stick to the routine. He wanted to capture the statistics in his logbook. He wanted to remain focused on his own quarry. He didn't want to miss the helicopter recovery of the spent first stage.

"Papa, come over here," Sean insisted.

"Ahh, alright." Albert gave a frustrated sigh as he obliged his son's innocent request.

Albert looked into his son's precision optic. What he saw surprised him. The image he viewed showed all five fairings were swirling like maple seeds. A slight condensation trail revealed a tornado-like vortex atop the front leading edge as the fairings spun like a helicopter rotor in auto-rotation. The leading-edge vortex lowered the air pressure over the twisted fairing's upper surface, effectively sucking the wing upward to oppose gravity. Four fairings in the set were spinning in a cluster together. Albert noted that the fairings weren't just falling. They were moving dramatically away, horizontally in a formation like migrating birds. They appeared to be attracted to the northwest as if pulled in that direction by an unseen force. The sight perplexed Albert.

An extended low rumble distinct from thunder engulfed Albert and broke his concentration. He stood back from the reticule. Sean took his place, resuming his view of the curious aerobatics, forgetting his obligation to record the arrival time of the sound wave.

"Stop the timer, Sean!" Albert shouted over the rockets' low rumble.

Sean ignored his father's instructions and panned his instruments to catch sight of the fifth fairing. He found it apart on its own. It was rotating as the others, but it wandered alone, separated from its flock to the north. It was on a solo trajectory, unaffected by whatever force attracted or guided the first set of four.

"What do you make of it, Papa? Where are the fairings going?"

Albert acquiesced to his son's innocent curiosity. He gave up on his own pursuit to indulge his young boy. He, too, found it odd that not once in all their research had they encountered any mention of the rocket fairings being reusable. He lost interest in the routine first stage recovery he was so eager to observe just a moment ago. Albert had never heard the New Zealand space agency or the Australian space agency advertise that any rocket's fairings were recoverable. He was a huge fan of Rockct Sci's reusability. Albert was sure it was a detail he would not have overlooked. He glanced at his logbook and did some mental math. The launches occur every 72 hours. He had records for at least 100 launches, two-thirds of which had twisty-cone fairings. Five fairings on each rocket would mean that this year alone, since he and Sean began to keep their records, over three hundred fairings would have fallen to the earth, and their records indicated that Rocket Sci could be on track for nearly 400 fairings before the end of the year. Surely other rocket launch aficionados like them would have reported some fairing recovery events. Why had they not heard of this?

"I don't know, son, I don't know." The elder said to his boy.

Sean kept his telescope trained to the north on the solo spinning fairing, wondering where it might reach the surface of the earth.

| Chapter 1 |

Water Dragon

Dubai. United Arab Emirates

The city skyline rose above the Persian Gulf shoreline like the emerald city of Oz. The cityscape sat in a heat, so solid even the trees had left for shade. The barren desert landscape around it in all directions made it seem as if the entire metropolis had been temporarily placed there until a more suitable location for the city could be found. Even the sea refused to hug the scorching beach sand. For over 60 years, since the mid-1980s, the Dubai Airshow has maintained worldwide prominence as a venue to showcase the future of aviation and space technology. The event is a must-attend for everyone in the aerospace industry. Dubai was an alien locale to Ethan Cross. He strode into the event hall's grand foyer with professional enthusiasm and proceeded to the biennial affair's check-in area. His company had sent him for the exposure the symposium offered to the cutting edge of autonomous flight control, and Cross thirsted for a new adventure.

The venue celebrated its 30th showing since its inception in 1986, with a holographic highlight reel of its most proud moments. Ethan Cross watched as the airport-style moving walkway glided him toward images of vintage commercial aircraft, which had headlined the show in years past. He recognized the antique Airbus

A380 and the venerable Boeing 787 Dreamliner, famous for its 25 years of routine 19-hour direct flight service spanning half the world from Sydney to London, a still popular lower-cost alternative to supersonic options. The translucent 3D projection reeled through impressive historic defense aircraft that had made appearances, like the sunsetted F-35 Joint Strike Fighter. It beamed images of retired spacecraft hardware like SpaceX's Dragon crew capsule, which used to take spacefarers to the space station. The fabled SpaceX Starship flashed next. Cross knew it was famous for having shuttled astronauts back to the moon and beyond when he was just a boy.

Ethan continued, propelled effortlessly by the gliding walkway surface and fueled by fascination. He found himself abeam of a holographic infomercial being cast in the middle of the purpose-built Dubai World Center foyer. He looked on as the prominent display materialized a massive white dragon—the creature towered above Cross. The ferocious-looking specimen lifted its jagged scaly head toward the raised cathedral ceiling of the venue's grand promenade. The scaly animal parted the thin lips of its long bird-like snout, revealing rows of razor teeth. The petrifying incisors lined its prehistoric beak. A dinosaur-like roar reverberated in the cavernous space as the dragon drew back its long white neck like a cobra snake coiled to strike. Cross was captivated by the scene unfolding before him as the walkway squared him off with the monster. A scattering of patrons who had been crossing the foyer stopped in their tracks in anticipation of Godzilla's next move. It lowered its snout, gazing down at Cross. It seemed to ignore the ant-like people below it. It was interested only in Cross. It craned and tilted its fierce head slightly to one side. Suddenly, it opened its mouth as a flaming hologram of fire ejected toward Cross. People in the foreground crouched, cowering from the faux attack's realism. The creature's vile head launched toward Cross, emerging through the plumb of flames. Its gaping mouth was opened wide, hurling at the walkway. It closed around Cross with a snap.

Cross blinked as the hologram vanished, morphing into a white, swan-like airplane. It was an image of this year's centerpiece attraction, an amphibious electric commuter jet designed and built by the Australian-Chinese venture, MagiX. They called it the Intellagama. The remarkable display confirmed what Ethan had heard about the name's meaning. A scale silhouette of the levitating plane landed in the sea as a holographic sun dropped below a virtual horizon behind it. Intellagama was Australian for Water-Dragon. The show concluded with hovering text; Intellagama: Sunset Forever after Eve. *Impressive advertisement,* thought Cross. A pang of adrenaline subsided in him as the escalator lifted him up and away.

Ethan had arrived a day early for the symposium. He finalized his check-in, electing to do so in person for the excuse to explore the famous venue. The trip was a boondoggle, a business trip that would be more play than work. The assignment was somewhat of a perk he had earned from his employer. Cross had opted to be sent to the airshow over some paid time off offered by his supervisor, Logan Kraft, to recognize Cross' extraordinary efforts in London at EV3. Cross preferred the more subtle thank you gesture over any public recognition or compensation alternatives.

Next, he was off to his hotel, another well-known location. He planned to enjoy a leisurely afternoon before the show would commence the following morning. Ethan stole a longing glance at the nearby vertiport as he hailed a ride share to the Jumeirah Beach Hotel, a wave-shaped structure built to complement the iconic sail-shaped Burj Al Arab Hotel nearby. Dubai's architecture was a cornucopia of uncoordinated themes, a theme park thesaurus of opulence excess.

Ethan peered out his electric ground taxi window with envy at the flying taxis overhead departing and approaching the vertiport autonomously. While flying taxis had become ubiquitous in Dubai, it was still a transportation mode of the well-to-do. Ethan's mind turned to thoughts of the Intellagama, another status symbol of the ultra-wealthy. It was state of the art. It was the pinnacle of what solar energy can offer, the possibility to go above and beyond what fossil fuel jet engines can do. Electric aircraft can fly at altitudes where the air is so thin; no internal combustion engine can operate. It boasted sustained long-range flight with zero carbon emissions. If that wasn't impressive enough, the Intellagama incorporated a hull design that enabled it to land on water. It was a flying boat, and it was a new must-have toy for the rich and famous, celebrities and corporate VIPs alike. It took the form of a silky business jet with sweeping bird-like wings that arched out elegantly like a swan, stemming from close to the hull's belly to above the top of the fuselage. The gull-like wings swooped tall to clear the water when touching down for an aquatic rendezvous. Like the Gulfstream G6's at the turn of the millennium, the Intellagama was frequently featured on popular posh periodicals like the Dupont Registry and the Rob Report. It enjoyed the occasional honorable mention in popular rap songs as a badge of wealth and unobtainium. It fit in well in this setting of overindulgence. MagiX hoped to bolster sales at the airshow, no different from every vendor present.

Ethan continued his daydream as he idly traced the paths of the airborne taxis overhead. He remarked to himself the cyclic nature of aviation technology. Over 100 years ago, in the late nineteen-thirties, Igor Sikorsky explored boundary-pushing configurations of flying boats at the industry's dawn. Some designs like the S-38 were coveted by aristocrats of the day, not unlike how the Intellagama is now. Sikorsky's S-38 was sometimes called "The Explorer's Air Yacht" as it had numerous private owners who received notoriety for their exploits. Then, as now, flying boats offer superior access to rural developing areas. When aircraft design was in its infancy, Sikorsky occupied himself with flying boats. In fact, a design innovation pioneered by Sikorsky himself was evident in the silhouette of the Intellagama. Midway down the bottom of the fuselage, a step in the boat hull was visible. The sudden jog in the otherwise clean mold line was a feature implemented by Sikorsky on the S-38 and other flying boats. It served to create cavitation that allowed the hull to break the surface tension of the water and lift off into the sky. Ethan marveled at the lasting mark one man could have on the evolution of an industry. Ethan knew that it wasn't until an engine with sufficient power-to-weight ratio came into being that Sikorsky could realize the vision he became most famous for, the rotary aircraft. Better known as the helicopter, Sikorsky's designs were the father to Dubai's hexacopter air taxis at which Ethan now gazed.

The parallel with Sikorsky's helicopter and the MagiX' Intellagama electric jet was two-fold. It became viable when its engine and power supply came into being. The Chinese-supplied power plant provided the necessary thrust enabling its unmatched range. Its unique solar panel technology supplied by another Australian company called NoviX provided the power needed for nearly endless sustained flight. Both technologies had come into maturity together, enabling MagiX to realize the Intellagama. The company offered a product that seemed as magic as the first helicopter seemed over 100 years ago, in 1939.

Two years before now, the plane famously left Perth at sunrise, headed west for 22,000 miles, and returned to Sydney before sunset 36 hours later, having stayed within the sunlight for the entire trip. That flight formed the basis for the aircraft's allure and formed the foundation of MagiX's enigmatic ethos; "Intellagama, sunset forever after eve."

The Intellagama promised unrestricted mobility, which is attractive to global business customers. It enjoys sales from corporate customers in remote rural China, where industry has expanded into the countryside faster than infrastructure contributing to the insatiable demand for energy and information, exacerbating the world's energy crisis. The Intellagama has a continent-traversing range and a water landing ability that provides unparalleled access. The unique solar cell technology is seamlessly integrated into each wing's upper contour and the hull's top surface. Collectively the panels produce almost all the energy consumed by its dual electric jet engines as it flies, making it capable of near-perpetual flight. It is a claim substantiated by MagiX's highly publicized sustained global traverse.

While he was impressed and intrigued by the pioneering machine as any aviation enthusiast, Ethan wasn't at the airshow to see the Itellagama. His company had sent him to the symposium for exposure to cutting-edge autonomous Man- Unmanned Teaming technology. The airshow always invited the latest in autonomous unmanned drone hardware. Dubai was renowned across the world as a hub for autonomous flight, having been the first to adopt and promote a network of flying taxis around the city. Ethan wanted to experience a flying taxi during his stay in the foreign land. He was eager for the novel experience, but he knew the convenience's premium price was not covered as an allowable expense on his business trip. Still, the windmills of his mind pondered how he might find an occasion for the experience while he was in Dubai for the airshow.

| Chapter 2 |

Feme Sole Trader

Jumeirah Beach, Dubai. UAE

Ethan emerged from the electric surface taxi at the Jumeirah Beach Hotel. He glanced at the searing sand of the venue's namesake. Baked by the day's relentless sunshine, the beach seemed to yearn for sunset. Ethan donned his stylish new comm-specs pressing the infrared-vis button on the frames as he dropped them over his eyes. With the infrared image augmenting his private view of the scene, he could view a section of the beach in front of the hotel that was significantly cooler than the surrounding terrain. It was where the subsurface refrigeration system strained against nature to extract enough heat from this tiny sliver of the gulf coast that a guest might be encouraged to lounge by the sea. The gimmick wasn't working. No one was on the sand. The air was so scorching, the soles of Ethan's shoes stuck to the light-colored pavement as he made his way for the hotel entrance.

The infrared-vis feature in his new comm-specs was working, however. Ethan was pleased with his recent purchase, despite this being the first time he had found any utility in the gimmick. The sophisticated sunglasses had their roots in military night vision technology. They were the latest selling feature of the newest generation of comm-specs, an internet access wearable with equivalent functionality to the ubiquitous comm-band.

Ethan had ditched his comm-band during escapades in London last year. Instead, his wrist was decorated with a handsome turquoise timepiece. A Pacific-centered map of the world adorned on its face. Ethan switched off his comm-specs' infrared vis feature to view the time. It was 5 pm. Good, he thought, time enough for a cold beer.

He proceeded to the nearby bar at Burj Al Arab Hotel. Its boat-like form was inspired by the sail of a dhow, a traditional Arabian sailing vessel used for fishing and pearling.

Ethan encountered a duo at the bar who were a few drinks into a one-up-manship conversation. Ethan took a seat a few vacant stools down from an attractive blonde woman who was keeping to herself across the bar from the sparring men. The pair of men were in heated debate and sat across the ellipse-shaped bar from the woman, speaking loudly so all could hear. Ethan perceived that the men were trying to outdo each other with impressive statements to attract the favor of the feme sole trader. Ethan viewed both the men and the woman from his stool near the ellipse-shaped bar top's apogee.

The first man with salty grey hair and matching beard remarked on the weather, "It's hot here in Dubai, no good for flying; after all, hot air is less dense than cool air."

The second man, who was clean-shaven, added, "At least we're at sea level. It would only be worse if we had this heat at a high altitude. High and hot, both poor conditions for flying"

Ethan surmised they were also staying in town for the airshow, judging by their conversation topic. He tipped the barman and downed a refreshing swig of the cold beer. Eavesdropping on the exchange was keeping him mildly entertained.

The salty-haired man added, "what we need is some humidity in this desert town. Denser air will be good for the airshow."

Ethan couldn't help but correct him. Politeness and social etiquette fell low on Ethan's priority when logic and fact were in jeopardy. Ethan interjected,

"Excuse me, but I can't help but point out the common misconception that humid air is more dense than dry air. Humid air is less dense. Hot and humid would make poor flight conditions for the show."

The salty-haired man immediately went on the defensive, "That can't be. If there is more water in the air, it's going to be denser."

"Not true," Ethan countered, "think of this bottle," Ethan motioned to his beer, "most people think that if you add water vapor to an empty bottle, you have more of something in there.

To make a given volume moister, you need to add water vapor molecules to the volume. To add water molecules to a bottle like this," Ethan rotated the artifact as he continued, "other molecules must be displaced." He took a quick sip and continued, "The pressure and temperature aren't changing, so any fixed volume of a gas has the same number of molecules."

"Yeah," said the well-kempt man taking sides with his former silver-haired adversary against their new common enemy, "but you just proved the point. It'll have the same number of denser water molecules."

Ethan fired another salvo of reason, "Dry air molecules weigh more than water molecules, which means that when a given volume is made moister by adding water molecules, heavier molecules become displaced by lighter water molecules. Therefore, moist air is lighter than dry air if nothing else changes."

The bearded man was unsure of himself now, "We are talking density of air, not the weight of molecules," He looked at his friend and then at the mysterious woman across the bar for some sign of approval. He hoped that somehow she too would take sides against his new come intruder.

Ethan launched a logic missile, "The amount of water vapor in the air also affects the density. Water vapor is a relatively light gas compared to Oxygen and Nitrogen in the air. Thus, when water vapor increases, the amount of Oxygen and Nitrogen decreases. The density decreases because mass is decreasing. So moist, humid air is bad for flying." Quod Erat Demonstrandum. Ethan took another swig of his beer and waited for a retort. None came from the defeated men, but Cross heard a soft clap.

The solo woman was smiling his way and gently tapping the fingers of one hand to the palm of her other. She stopped, picked up her beer bottle, stood, and walked toward Cross. She took a stool next to him. Cross was a sharp-looking man. With blue eyes, a masculine jawline, dark crew-cut hair that looked good even when it was mussed, and an athletic build, he didn't have difficulty getting a date. Still, Cross thought, 'This never happens,' as she sat and stuck out her hand.

"Alyne Jimmie." Cross detected a heavy Australian accent. It was a charming departure from the Northeastern American dialect to which he was accustomed.

"Ethan Cross." He flashed a blue-eyed smile, pleased with himself as the two challengers across the bar rose and moved to a table by the windows overlooking the Persian Gulf.

"You know your weather. Are you a pilot?" Alyne inquired as she leaned over the bar top holding up three fingers to the barman.

"No, I'm an.... I'm here for the airshow. You?" Cross

avoided telling her he was a defense contractor. He knew to be cautious of anyone who showed an interest in his job. From his career in the defense industry, he knew all too well that his Top Secret clearance status made him a target for espionage. In every security training video he had ever received, there would be a clip of the cliché seductress tempting the unwitting engineer with the high-level access. In each video, the woman was always a few points hotter than the dude. He wondered if a voyeur would recognize his current situation as that stereotypical engagement. More than that, he hadn't had much success picking up women by leading with his status as a flight control engineer. As she settled back onto the high-top seat next to his, he quickly traced the contour of the smart coral-colored business suit that flattered her feminine physique and instantly decided she was worthy of his best pick-up efforts.

"I'm here for the airshow as well." She continued. "I work for Rocket Sci. We launch out of New Zealand. Perhaps you've heard of us?" Cross had, and he knew the company launched small satellites. She continued before he responded, "I'm afraid our rockets would prefer those hot, humid conditions. Our launch commit criteria doesn't allow for launch in bad weather, but unlike an airplane, a rocket would perform better in thinner air" the barman placed three freshly opened cold bottles in front of the pair.

"That, I can't argue." He raised his bottle for a friendly toast with what was left of his beer. Her insightful comment caused Cross to reassess his initial stereotype of her. She was easy on the eyes, which led Cross to presume she was a marketing saleswoman or a booth babe for the trade show. Say what you will of equality, but Cross's observation was that corporations were wise to the power of a pretty face. Trade shows were often staffed with many of them. Alyne, however, seemed to have the intellect and charm to accompany her look. She put another beer down in front of him.

"Have another coldie; it's so hot you have to feed the chooks ice blocks, so they don't lay hard-boiled eggs 'round here," her Aussie slang amused Cross. Her Australian accent sounded like an exotic blend of a British spokes model and a truck driver from Down East.

"Thank you, yes. More ice blocks." Cross smiled at the phrase, "Did you hear that the beach is refrigerated?" Cross motioned casually across the room by tipping his beer toward the window. He looked past the two men shooting jealousy daggers with their eyes at Cross and his new companion.

"Really? Why am I not surprised? I hear they have an indoor ski area here. I want to take some turns before brekky one day this week- just to tell my mates back in Melbourne that I skied in the desert."

"You ski? Australia has ski areas?" Cross inquired.

"Nah Yeah, Straya has ski resorts. I grew up an hour from Mount Baw Baw. I used to try to make it to Mount Hotham at least once a season. We have had to drive 7 hours to Charlotte Pass the past few yonks to find any good pow. You ski then?"

"I do. North of Boston, there's plenty of good skiing. The most exotic destination I've skied though is in Europe at Ischgl in Austria, but I never thought of Australia as a ski destination."

"Skiing in Straya isn't exotic. Skiing in an Arabian desert, now that's exotic!" Alyne stuck out her bottle to cheer Ethan. Ethan obliged. "Well, it is decided then." She said, "A bushie and a yank will take some runs together in the big smoke of Dubai. Now that's a site. You from Boston then?" Ethan was enjoying the conversation. Her Aussie slang was quite endearing, and he was pretty sure she just asked him on a date. He knew to be cautious while on business travel of anyone interested in his occupation, but she hadn't asked about his work. Yet.

"Well," Cross smiled at her, "outside of Boston. I rounded to the nearest city." Alyne smiled over the top of her bottle.

He placed the cold oasis in his hand on the bar, rapidly formulating a discreet opinion of his friendly guest. He was attracted to her, for sure. She was personable. Check. He couldn't place her profession, but he knew Rocket Sci to be a reputable company. Ethan decided that she was a worthy investment of some of his discretionary time while in Dubai. Skiing indoors would be a great experience. He was cautiously optimistic about the outcome. Maybe she was single? Already he felt he wanted to spend more time with her. The frequency of travel that his job required afforded few opportunities to get to know someone. Familiarity breeds relationship, he thought, as he prepared to elaborate on his response to her earlier question.

He started to speak just as a dark-haired Asian man approached Alyne, put his hand on her back between her shoulder blades, and greeted her with a foreign attempt to replicate her Australian accent. "G'Day, Mate."

Alyne turned. With a familiar and enthusiastic smile, she offered her hand for a professional greeting, "G'Day, Mr. Chan. G'Day," Alyne turned back to the bar to grab the unattended third bottle. She was expecting him. Cross should have noticed when she ordered three drinks. Ethan felt a pang of disappointment. "Rick Chan, this is Ethan Cr..." Alyne paused to prompt Ethan to save her from the embarrassment of forgetting his full name. Ethan turned to Rick and stood from his barstool, offering a firm handshake.

"Ethan Cross." Rick stood a few inches taller than Ethan.

"Rick Chan, Solcom. You?"

Ethan answered with the conditioned indirect first-contact-with-a-foreign-stranger response that a seasoned defense contractor knew to apply, "I'm in Aerospace, here for the airshow," He paused, "and for the beach scene," Ethan motioned to the scorching empty beach.

Alyne flashed a smile of amusement at Ethan's clever response.

Alyne bolstered Rick's introduction, "Rick Chan is Chief Technical Officer of Solcom. His company is Rocket Sci's biggest customer. Rick and I work closely together," she paused, looking only at Rick.

"And we are sure to connect every other year at the event." Rick finished her sentence. She smiled pleasantly at her customer. Rick added, "It's the highlight of the show." He reached for her hand and kissed her fingers softly in an old-fashioned, strikingly non-Asian greeting. Rick had no detectable accent. In fact, he sounded American. His skin was light, and his features were more western than most Asians. "Where are you from, Mr. Cross?"

"I'm from the Northeastern U.S., and you?" Ethan's curiosity about the man's unique mix of traits compelled him to vector the conversation toward the newcomer. And he was curious about his relationship with Alyne. Ethan sat back on his stool as Rick adeptly slid another between Ethan and Alyne and seated himself.

"Wuhan China, originally. I did my undergrad at the University of Technical Sciences. I finished my first thesis in the States, though, Austin, Texas." Rick chuckled proudly at his own accomplishment. Alyne laughed politely. Cross thought, *First Thesis?* No one had asked about Rick's schooling. Cross rarely mentioned his own Ivy League background as to him it seemed superfluous in most conversations and unbecoming. Ethan wasn't a fan of the man's arrogance, but he gave him the benefit of the doubt.

"First thesis?" Ethan indulged Rick's remark, "You've written more than one?"

"My first Ph.D. was in communications networks. My second Ph.D. was in nano-manufacturing."

"That's no small feat." Ethan flashed another blue-eyed smile at Alyne, who smirked. She got the joke.

Rick didn't seem amused. Alyne spoke next, "Rick's company has done nearly 100 launches with Rocket Sci this year. That's more than the Australian and New Zealand governments have launched with us this year combined."

"What sort of payload are you launching that frequently?" Ethan inquired with genuine interest.

"Communications satellites. Solcom is building a network of low earth orbit satellites to offer global internet services, with a focus on the people of rural mainland China. We service the Australian market as well." Rick said proudly.

"Just Like Amazon's Kuiper, or Space X's Starlink constellation that's been in service for over two decades?" Ethan offered a passive-aggressive fact to put him in his place. A LEO constellation for internet service wasn't unique. And what a strange way to say that, *with a focus on the people of rural mainland, odd*, thought Cross.

"Yes and no. Our Icarus constellation offers a similar service, but it's sovereign to China, not reliant on a US-based infrastructure. It's different than Starlink because all the satellites are interconnected via optical communication cross-links."

"You mean lasers?" Ethan asked

"Yes, Laser communications offer low latency, high bandwidth data transfer. Our initial constellation boasts some of the fastest downlink speeds ever for a satellite-based internet service."

"Downlink? As in from space to the ground? Your satellites are interconnected by lasers, but also to the ground?"

"The downlink is our discriminating technology. We aren't the only ones using laser cross-links, but getting volumes of data to the ground distinguishes our service from any other. People demand the fastest download speeds. They can tolerate a slower upload but a slow stream, and they'll go to another service provider, given a choice."

"And you're here at the show to size up the competition?" Ethan knew the airshow's symposium would showcase a myriad of Sat-Com companies and their latest wares.

"No, I'm here for the Intelagama. There has never been an aircraft like it!" Rick said, glowing with enthusiasm.

Alyne picked up on his excitement, "I hear it can land on water."

"Yes," Said Rick, "but the solar panels are the tech that impresses me most."

"Not the electric jet engines? They are a Chinese design, are they not?" Ethan's flight controls background would give him an advantage in the discussion, he thought, if he could steer the Intellagama conversation to the engines.

"Yes, they are. I appreciate the Intellagama's electric jet engine; after all, as you mention, they are an evolution of a concept demonstrated first in 2020 by researchers at my Alma Mater, Wuhan University."

Ethan interjected. "I understand it compresses air and ionizes it using microwaves, generating plasma that thrusts the engine forward."

Rick responded. "Yes, my government licensed the technology to Australia for use by MagiX. It's impressive indeed, but it is only half of the architecture that enables the jet's impressive performance. The solar panels are the true magic. They are supplied by another Australian venture called NoviX. I hope that the Australian government will license the technology to Solcom in kind. Quid-pro-Quo for the electric jet engine technology in the Intellagama." It didn't appear to Ethan as if Rick was about to stop.

"NoviX perfected a design that captures and converts more energy more efficiently from the sun. Nearly four times more efficiently, in fact, than the common photovoltaic cells that permeate the rooftops of homes and businesses across the world. NoviX designs use carbon nanotubes to achieve nearly 90% energy conversion from sunlight versus approximately 20% for traditional photovoltaic solar cells. The cells convert electricity from the ultraviolet, the visible, and infrared part of the spectrum. NoviX cells offer performance that rivals the likes of photosynthesis." Rick laughed at his own nerd joke. Alyne encouraged him. Ethan took a sip of his beer.

"I hear the Intellagama flew non-stop around the World," Alyne kept Rick fueled by her volley.

Rick was informed of the well-publicized accomplishment. "Almost around the world. They left Perth, headed west, and returned to Sydney. The Earth's circumference at low latitudes is less than at the equator. Still, it's an impressive record nonetheless."

Ethan offered, "For such a capable aircraft, it seems restrictive that it can't fly in the dark" The comment was intended to be a joke, but there was too much truth in it for the humor to win over the practicality of the statement. Rick addressed Ethan's observation.

"The aircraft is sold in a corporate configuration, which includes the option for a high-density battery that offers a few hours of flight at night. However, it's a bit of a performance hit due to the weight. The Intellagama doesn't have a limitless range with the battery option, nor can it fly as high. Instead, the battery affords flight in poor weather conditions and enables flight in the dark. One can opt, however, for the Intellagama Explorer edition that doesn't compromise its range when operated in the daytime, which trades the weight of the batteries, for a lighter payload; a boat."

"A boat?" Alyne inquired, "Isn't the whole airplane a boat when it lands on the water?"

"Yes, it is, my dear," Rick addressed Alyne with a phrase more familiar than Ethan would have expected for a relationship between business partners, "but how often might you be in need of a dinghy any time you land on a remote lake?" Rick asked a rhetorical question, "MagiX has thought of everything. It's a remarkable machine. I want one. Besides, who wants to fly at night, anyway? You'll miss all the sights." Rick took a quick swig of his bottle and spoke again before either of his companions had a chance. "Speaking of night and sights, what sights can we take in this fine town tonight?"

Alyne spoke up without hesitation, "Ethan and I were just talking about hitting the slopes one morning. They have an indoor alpine ski area here in Dubai. Wild, right?"

"Yes, I've heard. The morning? Why wait? Let's all go...Right now. I'll have my assistant bring my skis to the venue at once." Rick snapped his fingers, and a bald Polynesian man wearing sunglasses inside stepped closer to the trio in response to Rick's hail. Ethan thought, wow, a double Ph.D., with an assistant, who travels to a city in a desert with his own pair of skis, just in case? He was beginning to dislike Rick for his egotism, or maybe because he had spoiled his ski date with Alyne. Ethan could feel a mild wave of jealousy pass through him. How could he win Alyne's favor over a globetrotting CTO? Ethan thought, let's see who is better on the slopes.

| Chapter 3 |

Desert Slalom

The indoor ski area's foyer was like an airlock to another world. A massive wall of glass windows separated the bustling Emirates shopping mall's familiar conditioned air from an expansive snow-scaped arctic climate. On the far side of the glass, the group looked up to view the distant pastel blue ceiling and the walls above and beyond snow-covered ski slopes lining the alien terrain. The room where they readied themselves for the escapade was part ski lodge, part gift shop, and part gymnasium locker room. Rick had just paid the rental bill for Alyne and Ethan's ski boots, skis, poles, and ugly multi-colored winter parkas, decorated in the national hues of the United Arab Emirates: red, green, white, and black.

Rick's quiet assistant stood nearby, holding a pair of high-end skis and poles at the ready for Rick. Rick boasted of his superior foresight as he donned a stylish orange and white jacket he had delivered for the occasion, "You never know when you might find yourself in the middle of the desert in need of a winter coat." Rick's humor came across as more pompous than witty. "I thought I might find an opportunity to get a few turns in on this trip, so I had my ski gear sent along" Rick took the polished orange skis from his shaded assistant without acknowledging the man. "I do hope the rentals offer you a satisfactory experience." Rick pointed out his generosity as he inspected the finer craftsmanship of his enviable pair of alpine shape skis.

Alyne politely responded to the subtle prompt, "Thank you, Rick. It was very generous of you to pick up the tab for our equipment." Alyne stood from the bench she shared with Ethan and turned to Ethan with another polite expression of gratitude.

"And thank you, Ethan, for these sporty gloves and memorable Ski-Dubai hat," She smiled at him as she pulled on the hideously colored red, green, white, and black colored gloves. Ethan donned his matching hat as he stood in his poorly fitted rental boots.

"You're welcome, Alyne; this tourist trap didn't give us much variety in style selection. At least they match these posh winter coats." Cross smiled with sarcasm.

"Not to worry, mate. This is one bizarre business excursion. What's the most bizarre business trip experience you've ever had? Anything that can top this?"

Ethan recalled his recent stint in London. So much about that trip would qualify. The chamber escapes the wicked plot, the sinister deception. How could he even begin to describe or put context with any of it? He answered with sarcasm;

"I once had to escape a dungeon and evade the clutches of an evil corporate mastermind who was chasing me across London with a deadly drone. I escaped with some secret intelligence about a mysterious product," said Ethan, knowing the sensational account would sound like a made-up answer. Alyne laughed at what she thought was a fabricated response. Sometimes, truth is stranger than fiction.

"Wow, that was a hell of a day at the office—that sounds like the plot of Sherlock Holmes. You'll have to explain that one later." Alyne said, "I once had to kickbox my way out of a meeting. Wrap your laughing gear 'round that."

"Kickbox, there's got to be a good story behind that too," Cross expressed interest in the back story. "Rick, and you?"

Rick responded, "My greatest business challenges have been Mergers and Acquisitions...."

'Yawn,' thought Cross. He elected to be cordial anyway

"Rick, thank you again for the tickets. I hope you'll allow me to repay you with a round of après ski- hot cocoas?" Cross said jokingly.

Alyne laughed again at Ethan's cute gesture. It wasn't an offer of equivalent value, but the humbling offer was endearing nonetheless. Cross was happy that he had made her smile.

Rick led the way through a double set of glass doors into the colossal snow globe. Cross and Alyne cobbled behind across the thick rubber-lined surface of the portal. Ethan felt a familiar icy crunch as they crossed the threshold, and his boots left prints in crisp white snow.

The trio approached a quad chairlift that hung from the ceiling. There was no necessity for towers to support the series of pulleys that suspended the chairlift cable. Instead, the Rube Goldberg mechanism hung from the roof above in a Doctor Seuss – looking arrangement. The chairlift began its 85-meter long ascent in front of them. Cross looked up to the top of the indoor mountain. The fabricated terrain veered to the left as it rose and terminated at a height equivalent to a 25-story building. Cross was inside the world's most massive freezer. The resort advertised five slopes of varying steepness and difficulty, including a 400-meter-long run, and boasted the world's first indoor black diamond trail. Despite its grandeur, the impressive scene looked like a bunny slope to Cross.

There was hardly anyone else on the slopes this late at night. The trio took their places in the boarding stalls awaiting a string of waist-level red LEDs to flash green, releasing the barrier and signaling they were clear to advance to the next chair. They occupied three of the four loading ports, each of which had a pair of opposing paddles that reminded Cross of the swinging saloon doors of an old western speakeasy. Cross stole a glance at Chan, who had taken the middle stall between Cross and Alyne. Chan caught Ethan's look and gave a side-eyed smirk; the duel was on. Cross' competitiveness surged as the loading stall light-emitting diodes flashed green, and the starting gate opened.

Chan started the conversation as the chair lifted their feet from the unnatural desert snow.

"MagiX is here with the Intellagama. I can't wait to see the plane in person tomorrow at the airshow. Did you know that NoviX, the supplier to MagiX, has developed a technology that generates the cleanest and cheapest form of energy on Earth."

Ethan knew that statement to be false, but the Top Secret nature of his contrary knowledge prohibited him from challenging the information. Rick continued, "The flexible cells convert light to electricity from the entire solar spectrum. Its carbon nanotube (CNT) antennas are small enough to match the nano-scale wavelengths of sunlight. NoviX CNTs can convert the electromagnetic spectrum much more efficiently than the best photovoltaic cells."

"How do they accomplish that?" Alyne asked.

"NoviX invented and manufactures the world's fastest diode – a critical component for energy conversion."

The chair they were on entered the midway station where a passenger could choose to get off partway up the slope. Cross couldn't fathom why. The entire structure paled in stature to even the most modest real mountain. Alyne invited Chan to continue with another question that appealed to his academic interests.

"How does a typical Solar Panel work?" she inquired.

Rick continued with enthusiasm, unphased by the slight left-hand trajectory change that their suspended chair apparatus made at the midway station as it continued to shuttle them up the artificial hill.

"Traditional solar technology is based upon the photovoltaic effect that was first shown more than 200 years ago in 1839. In a Photovoltaic (P.V.) solar cell, when a photon approaches an electron and has the energy level needed, it can be absorbed by the electron. That, in turn, excites the electron, moving it to a higher energy state and breaking it free to flow as electricity. Channeling the free electrons creates an electric current that can power a device.

The trouble with P.V. technology is that not just any photon can excite an electron. The photon needs to have a minimum amount of energy. That means that lower-energy infrared light, which is about 40% of all solar energy to hit the Earth's surface, is not used in a traditional solar cell to generate electricity. Furthermore, only certain frequencies, or specific colors of light that correspond to the energy states, can knock an electron free. Of course, a weak light cannot excite an electron to the next higher energy state, so dim lights produce zero power in P.V. cells. All of this limits the efficiency of P.V.

solar cells to around 20% max. By comparison, NoviX carbon nanotube panels have a theoretical efficiency limit of 90%, which opens the door for applications like the Intellagama."

It was curious to Cross that the CTO of a telecommunications company would have so much interest in an energy generation technology like solar panels. Cross could see Alyne listening intently to Chan's dissertation.

"I'm still not getting how NoviX nanotech works?" Alyne said. Chan had her full attention.

Like the sparring men at the bar, Ethan beat Chan to the response, offering Alyne an analogy to decode Chan's tech talk.

"Think of NoviX's solar panels like this. Imagine a grand piano with the back open and its strings exposed. Imagine the sun's rays are represented by a flash light beam cast over all the strings. White light, like sunlight, contains all the colors of the visible spectrum. Sunlight also includes ultraviolet and infrared light on either side of the visible band. Let's call them the high and low notes. Now, imagine the strings are NoviX's carbon nanotubes, and each one responds to a different color or frequency. If the piano were tuned to be like a traditional P.V. solar cell, it would play only the notes in the middle corresponding to visible light when the flashlight shines across the strings. Every note will play, low to high, if it's tuned to be like a NoviX solar cell. With a rectifying circuit at the end of each string, you can make a lot more energy from the NoviX piano. It might sound terrible, but it's MagiX, really." Ethan winked at Alyne.

"Naw, Yeah, I get it now! And that's how the Intellagama makes enough energy to fly. Thanks, Ethan!" Alyne said happily. Ethan turned to Chan, continuing his conversational triumph with some aviation history.

"Thirty years ago, in 2016, the Swiss Solar Impulse project did what the Intellagama has done. It was the first fixed-wing solar aircraft to circumnavigate the Earth. And another Swiss eco-entrepreneur, Raphaël Domjan, achieved a first in his SolarStratos sometime around 2023 when he soared epically to the edge of space at 60000 feet in the first commercial solar-powered aircraft. Domjan was inspired to make the SolarStratos aircraft after earning some notoriety from sailing his solar boat around the world. "

"A solar boat and a solar plane? Maybe," Alyne responded enthusiastically, "Domjan's pioneering solar expeditions in the air and the sea inspired the Intellagama's designers at MagiX's to pursue an amphibious craft?" she said smiling. Cross' trivia had stolen her attention from Chan. Cross smiled back.

Rick turned the party's attention away from the academic exchange with a sudden observation.

"Bar up! We've reached the top." The Intellagama conversation was cut short by the chairlift's arrival at the summit.

Alyne adeptly slipped off the chair and skied ahead of the men. Chan glanced at Cross, impressed. Cross acknowledged with an approving nod. The men coasted to where she had hockey-stopped at the top of the slope. She wasn't exaggerating her time on skis. A slalom course had been set on the slope ahead of them.

"You boys gonna let a Sheila out do ya? Can you keep up with my Baw Baw backside on this corduroy piste?" Alyne charged ahead with a strong push-off from well-planted poles. She entered the slalom gates and skillfully navigated the first few. Her unflattering square-cut rental jacket failed to mask her feminine form as she carved left, then right, and left again, smacking the gates with alternating gloved fists as she leaned tightly into her turns. She cleanly cleared about a dozen gates before exiting the course about halfway down, skiing out and looking up at the boys from just under a medium-sized jump positioned near the course. She slid to a stop and beckoned them to come.

Chan gestured to Cross to proceed first. "Have at it, hoss," he said with a southwest American slang he robbed from his time in Austin, no doubt.

It was a welcome invitation. Good, thought Cross. I'll give him a run he won't soon match. Cross skated three or four times, pushing off the snow with each stride, and entered the course with speed. Cross gauged the slope to be mild. It was a novice course, and he was crushing his first few turns through the gates. The jump appeared to the right of his field of vision, a half a dozen gates ahead. He could see Alyne watching his progress below. He had reached a comfortable rhythm. He felt the low-quality boots push back against his shins. His downhill edges seemed to hold well as he executed each turn's apex just above each approaching gate. His days of ski racing triggered muscle memory: outside, inside, outside. Cross made a game-time decision to exit the course a few gates earlier than Alyne had to square off with the jump. He came out of the last gate balanced for a trick he knew well. He coiled his body and arms to his right like winding a clock spring. As his ski tips kissed the base of the jump, he released, twisting his torso counter-clockwise while turning his head as far as he could over his left shoulder. He pushed up off the top of the jump. His body followed his head in a high, slow pirouette called a helicopter. The landing came a fraction of a second sooner than Cross anticipated, but he stuck it with only a slight balance check after a full 360-degree rotation. He finished just upslope of Alyne, spraying her below the waist with a playful burst of snow from a cleanly executed hockey stop. She smiled widely as Ethan drank in the après adrenaline rush.

The pair looked up to Rick with a collective hail for him to proceed. Cross proudly thought to himself, beat that Doctor Wuhan Wonton.

Rick launched strongly into the course. He skated to the first gate and punched it down powerfully. He crisply set for the next gate and then the next. He looked like an orange zipper trolley sewing up two halves of a racing bodysuit. Rick exited the gauntlet at the same gate where Cross had earlier. Chan pressed against the snow with three quick skates to gain even more momentum for the jump. At the last moment, Rick spun 180 on his skis and hit the jump switch. He finished a full rotation in the air and landed backward as well. He completed his flawless run uphill of Cross with enough momentum to spray Cross in the face with a fist of icy snow.

"Not bad for an old Doctor, huh?"

This guy was as full of himself as a fighter pilot. Ethan couldn't hold his tongue. He pushed forward on his poles and turned 180 to face his companions as he wiped the snow from his face, using the back of his glove.

"How do you know if there is a doctor in the house?" Ethan said flatly.

Chan took the bait, "I don't know, how?"

"He'll tell you." Ethan gave Alyne a blue-eyed wink and skied ahead as a smirk formed on her almond-shaped rosy face. Cross didn't wait for Chan's reaction as he pointed his ski tips downhill and set off for the base.

Just as he reached the bottom of the slope, Ethan's comm-specs alerted him to an incoming call. A miniature transparent portrait of a well-groomed grey-bearded face appeared with text below it on his shades' inside surface. Logan Kraft. Ethan immediately changed his focus from the competitive escapade. His attention turned entirely to the incoming message from his mentor and supervisor. It was 3 pm on a Sunday back home. Why was Logan calling him? It must be urgent for a Vice President and General Manager of a large defense contractor to call on a Sunday. Usually, when Logan called Ethan, it was to put him onto a tough technical assignment that he trusted no one else to solve. Cross figured it was important for him to reach out to Cross, knowing Ethan was away on business travel. Cross tapped the call button on the top of his comm-specs' right-hand ear-stay. Logan began to speak as Ethan greeted him; they spoke over each other awkwardly. "Good afternoon, Logan."

"Good evening, Ethan." Ethan let his elder continue, "It's late there, I know. I hope I haven't woken you" Ethan glanced back at the slopes, his hand still on the earpiece. Alyne was looking his way. He motioned with his pointer finger while still grasping both ski poles to his other hand over his ear. Alyne watched him and nodded with a smile, acknowledging that he had received a phone call. Ethan watched her turn and board the next chair lift with Rick. A slight twinge of jealously stung him as he responded to Logan.

"No worries, sir, how can I help you?" Ethan offered a genuine salute to his superior.

"I'm at a quandary. I've been asked to answer some questions for a close friend, and they are on a subject that requires your unique expertise." Logan had an uncanny way of making Ethan feel important. Ethan had a stellar track record for solving challenging problems for the company, mainly in the area of flight controls. Some years ago, his work on the CENTURI drone formation flight protocol had earned his company notoriety in the technical community for expertise in autonomous flight controls. His recent experience investigating the ARCELOR had given Ethan near-celebrity status with Logan, one of the few people on the planet who was fully aware of the impacts of Ethan's work due to the secret compartmentalized nature of the job. His success there had earned him this very trip to the Dubai Airshow. "I know how much you have been looking forward to the airshow, and you've earned it, but I'm afraid my request may have to interrupt your experience. Would that be ok?"

"Of course, what is it?" Ethan was no stranger to burning the midnight oil. He was confident he could work on any technical problem and still attend parts of the airshow.

"I need you to travel to troubleshoot a...." Logan paused to choose his words, "a piece of hardware that my colleague at the Reagan Missile Range is in possession of." The request started to sound like Ethan would have to take a rain check on the airshow. Ethan exited the giant snow globe and stopped his lumbering ski-boot-footed stride in the gift shop in front of a giant glass window overlooking the fabricated winter scene. To his left was Rick Chan's assistant, who was patiently watching his boss enjoy himself with Alyne Jimmie through his dark-shaded comm-specs. Ethan exchanged an impersonal sunglass-to-sunglass nod with the puzzling Polynesian man as he continued his conversation with Logan.

"What sort of hardware?" Ethan asked

"It's a solar panel that has been recovered from the sea" That was a statement that needed unpacking.

"A solar panel recovered from the sea?" Ethan repeated, prompting Logan to elaborate.

"Well, perhaps more accurately, recovered from a spacecraft and found in the ocean," Logan's progressive elaboration was certainly piquing Ethan's curiosity.

"A solar panel recovered from a spacecraft?" Ethan repeated, "I can't imagine how a solar panel could survive the extreme heat of reentry through the atmosphere. Are you certain it came from a spacecraft?"

"Yes, Ethan, there are some particular features that make the specimen a...." Logan paused again, "a curiosity. It is unlike any solar array my colleague has encountered. He's been studying it for a couple of weeks and has discovered some other interesting attributes that he cannot explain."

"Attributes like what?" Ethan inquired.

"It has a control surface, like the trailing edge of an airplane wing. My colleague has identified what he believes to be an electronic flight control box and has accessed a flight control algorithm of some sort. He can't make heads or tails of it. That's when he called me, and it's why I'm calling you. You're our leading expert on the topic."

"Fascinating. Is the solar panel shaped like a wing? How do you know it's from a spacecraft? A spacecraft wouldn't need a wing-shaped panel. "

Logan elaborated, "The panel is not an aircraft wing, although it looks a bit like a misshapen windmill blade. The solar cells are built into the surface of a rocket nose cone fairing."

"A rocket nose-cone fairing? Aren't those usually discarded when a second stage releases its contents? An aeroshell typically wouldn't make it into space unless it was designed to be part of the payload to be delivered to orbit."

"It's not like that, Ethan. It's even more bizarre. The solar panel is installed on the inside surface of the fairing. It has a slightly concave shape and follows the inner contour of the shell" Ethan's mind was working at full tilt.

"That doesn't make any sense. How could that be useful when enclosed on the tip of a rocket? Does it look like it is designed to remain on-orbit?"

"I haven't seen it myself, but I asked the same thing.

My associate assured me that electronics don't appear to be radiation-hardened or space-qualified. He did say it was quite the task to gain access to the internals. After all, it was sealed up well enough to survive floating on in the Pacific for who knows how long."

"The Pacific? Where exactly was it found?"

"Have you ever heard of the Ronald Reagan Ballistic Missile Defense Test Site?"

"No, but it sounds like it would be out west in Nevada somewhere. No ocean there."

"No. It's in the Marshal Islands, Central Pacific. A couple of thousand miles south of Hawaii. Fifteen hundred miles east of Guam."

"Sounds remote."

"It is. Geographically, it may be the most distant strip of land from any continent, which is why it was chosen as a test site for nuclear and hydrogen bombs almost one hundred years ago."

"Ok. Do we know where the rocket it came off of was launched from?"

Logan hesitated, "Yes, but I'd rather not say on an open line. I've emailed some additional details to you at your company email. I would encourage you to review that message at your earliest convenience. I'd really value your impressions as soon as you review them. I'd like to pass them along and confirm your arrival with my associate there when I receive your reply" Ethan knew that Logan never gave a direct order. Despite carrying the positional authority to do so, Logan always employed a leadership style of indirect suggestion and encouragement. He gave Cross a reputation to live up to. It was a style that President Lincoln was famous for employing when giving direction to his generals, like Ulysses Grant. Ethan knew that Logan's request to review the message was as direct an order as he'd ever received. He would have to soldier onto his hotel to check his email immediately following this call.

"Ethan, I should mention that I anticipate this artifact, and any investigation surrounding it will soon become classified. Shortly after contacting me, my colleague reported the finding up his change of command to the Missile Space Intelligence Center (MSIC) in Huntsville. He told me that he felt that too much time had elapsed between when it was recovered and when he contacted me to delay the report any longer. I advised him to wait for your onsite evaluation before calling in the find, but he went ahead with the report through his established channels shortly after speaking with me. I expect some sort of security class guide to be established imminently, so I'm telling you what I know now, but be ready to report back via secure access channels when you arrive." Ethan started to feel the gravitas of the request. When you arrive – It sounded like travel plans had already been made on his behalf. Logan had made it seem like Ethan had a choice in his symposium interruption, but Ethan sensed the assignment had already been arranged.

"So let me sum this up. You have a friend who lives on an island in the middle of the Pacific Ocean, who has happened upon a piece of space debris floating in the sea, and you want me to go to a defunct nuclear test site to check it out?"

"That about sums it up, yes. I might add, there is some urgency for you to get there. MSIC is sending a couple of reps, and the National Security Agency will likely send an agent, and even the folks from Alice Springs got wind of the recovery. I suspect they'll be sending some personnel too. There is a battle over the jurisdiction and whether to return it at all, as the space debris treaty established in 1967 would suggest. Since you're already halfway around the globe, you have a head start on the U.S. contingent, and you very well may arrive first. I'm hoping you'll get there in time to work with it before it gets subsumed by the bureaucracy."

"Well, then, what are we waiting for?"

"We aren't waiting. Christine has made arrangements for you to leave on the first available flight out of Dubai tomorrow, Monday. The itinerary is in your inbox. You're on the first flight east. It will depart at about local 3 pm tomorrow. I know that this assignment in Dubai was meant to be an opportunity to unwind, and well deserved, I might add. I'm afraid you'll have to wait a couple of years for the next airshow. How can I make it up to you?" Ethan didn't feel that any consolation compensation was necessary. He was happy to be asked to help with something so important to Logan. Ethan wondered what the relationship was that Logan had with his point of contact at the test site. He wondered how long it would take to get there. He wondered if he could even offer anything more once he arrived. He had many questions, but one struck him in response to Logan's inquiry.

"Well, sir, would you allow me to take a sky taxi to catch my flight at the airport?"

"Ha. Ha. Is that all you want? Yes, Ethan. I'll be sure to approve the expense. And thank you for giving up your airshow experience. I'm in your debt as usual. Any other questions before we speak again?"

"Yes. Who is my Point of Contact when I arrive? Your colleague knows I'm coming at your request?"

"Ah, yes. It's also in the message, but his name is David Archie Dodge. He is an old college friend. We were undergrad roommates for a time at MIT. He's a character – a Ph.D. in radio systems, a bit of a mad scientist, and a tinkerer. And he's a real...." Logan's photo in the corner of the glass was only a still profile, but Logan paused enough for Ethan to sense his mentor smile through his comm-specs. "He's a real ham." Logan chuckled. "Don't believe any of the stories he tells you about me. I told him about you, and he's expecting you."

"Ok. Great. I'll take a look at your message."

"Thank you, Ethan. I know you'll make us proud; you always do. Good luck, but you won't need luck." Logan ended the call; his image in Cross' comm-specs persisted for a moment and then vanished from view.

Cross wanted to say goodbye to Alyne, but she and Rick had ascended well out of sight. He didn't feel he had the time to wait for her and Rick to ski down. Perhaps he could find her at the show in the morning before he had to depart? He was jealous that Rick was alone with her. Cross remembered Rick's awaiting assistant nearby. He took a pace toward the bald man, still unsure if he spoke or even fully understood English, and said,

"Excuse me, would you kindly pass my regards to your boss and Miss Jimmie? There are some matters I must attend to." Ethan hoped he might run into Alyne again in the morning at the show before he had to depart.

The bald man squared off to Ethan, touched the tips of his fingers together, and nodded at Cross in a bow of acknowledgment. He said nothing. As he bent and lowered his head, his sleeves pulled back, revealing an intricate tattoo of a dragon with a serpent-like scaled tail. Cross wondered if something had been lost in translation. He waved a thank you and departed in the direction of duty.

| Chapter 4 |

The Skai

Cross paused at the threshold of a grand auditorium to search for a vacant chair. He checked his watch. He had about 30 minutes to spend at the show before he would have to leave for the Airport. He hoped to catch the opening address. The keynote was always a noteworthy part of a trade show. The speaker was sure to provide a thematic kickoff and perhaps offer a preview of the week that Cross would now have to miss. He scanned the auditorium for an empty seat as he advanced into the cavernous space, secretly hoping he might spot Alyne in the crowd. She was nowhere in view. It was a long shot. He wondered if he'd have time to swing by Rocket Sci's booth in the convention hall? She was sure to be there. He found an empty chair at the end of a row. Cross released his black backpack's orange grip handle, setting it down between his legs as he took a seat.

A series of photos cycled on the backdrop of the empty stage. Cross recognized the Intellagama flying boat in a few of them as he waited. Another ten minutes passed before there was any sign of activity ahead of him. Soon, an attractive woman, dressed smartly in a tailored coral-colored business suit, took the stage. She strode to the center of the platform and stopped behind a glass podium. The woman addressed the symposium audience to kick off the biennial event.

"Good Morning. I'm Alyne Jimmie, Rocket Sci's Launch and Mission Integration Director. We are celebrating 60 years of showcasing the best of the aerospace industry. Welcome to the 30th Dubai airshow.

Newer, more advanced technologies will naturally replace older, less useful ideas. Gone are the days of disposable space launch systems. Rocket Sci prides itself on nearly full reusability. We recover our first stage rockets using a combination of aero-thermal deceleration and helicopter Fulton capture. Our launch facility at the Mahia Peninsula is the best spot in the world for launching more frequently than anywhere else on the planet. Rocket Sci can launch every three days from the east coast of New Zealand's North Island, supporting 120 launches per year. From there, rockets can reach a variety of orbits around the Earth — from near-polar sun-synchronous orbits to 39 degrees....."

Ethan was impressed. Alyne was not just a pretty face. He was embarrassed that he had pegged her for a booth babe. As it turns out, she was an orbital mission director. She continued her speech.

"We can take any period in history and observe that newer, more advanced technologies will naturally replace older, less useful ideas. It's a constant that is engrained in each of us. New replaces used, young replaces old, the evidence is as natural as seasons change. Progress is made...."

Her speech was engaging. Cross wished he could stay longer. He looked at the face of his watch. A Pacific-centered map of the world stared back at him as if reminding him of the location of his following obligation. No time. He would have to miss the end of Alyne's address. He slipped politely out of his seat, passing by rows of airshow patrons, their eyes glued to the stage. He unclenched his grip on his pack's orange handle as he swung the small black backpack adeptly over one shoulder, thankful that he always traveled light. In it, he carried just essentials; his comm-pad, some business attire, and a bathing suit. Cross headed out to the vertiport area where vacant air taxis awaited fares.

Cross recognized the air-taxi as the Skai Hydrogen-powered hexacopter from the Massachusetts Company, Alaka'i. It was first fielded around 2025. The sleek-looking 20-year-old hexacopter aircraft, designed by BMW Designworks for Alaka'i, still looked modern. Its timeless design had become an icon of the city. Dubai was known for the massive investment it had made in a hydrogen infrastructure to support the adoption of the hydrogen fuel cell-powered air taxis. Cross approached and entered the nearest craft at the prompt of an attendant at the threshold of the flight line. He sat in a stylish bucket seat that reminded him of a sports car. He rotated the clasp of a four-point harness as a clear glass door closed autonomously behind him. He remarked to himself how much trust he put into technology as the hexacopter lifted him from the tarmac and yawed on a vector to the Dubai international airport.

He was the sole occupant of the pilotless transport. Powerful electric motors on each arm of the rotorcraft quietly propelled Cross away from the airshow he had been so excited to attend. He would have liked to stay for the airshow, but the aerial departure nearly made up for it. Cross considered himself fortunate, knowing that Dubai is the only place where the unique fuel cell-powered aircraft operated. Due to the high infrastructure expense, hydrogen-based electric power generated from fuel cells was minimally used in air transportation applications worldwide. It was the only place one could have such a posh experience. The unique look of the Skai had become synonymous with the city, much like the Hackney carriage taxis or electric black-cabs were iconic to London.

Cross' thoughts took him back to London for a moment. His mind flashed to another novel power source he had encountered there. A twinge of aggravation started to grip him. He shook the memory, as he had done so many times before. He was back in Dubai to appreciate the moment.

Aside from the famous Dubai air taxis, fuel cells remained relegated to just a few specialized aerospace applications. Most famously, NASA's space shuttle used a fuel cell as far back as 65 years ago because of the utility of the potable water that the chemical reaction exhausted. Fuel cells combine Hydrogen gas stored onboard with Oxygen gas, usually right out of the air, through a process that yields electricity and pure water. The Skai simply expelled its water waste into the heat of the desert, where it sublimed into vapor before ever raining down onto the streets of the Emerald City below. It was a clean, high-end transportation method for its high-class occupants to boast about to their high-class friends. Cross felt out of his element as he passed through the opulent skyline.

The Skai was powered by one of the most environmentally friendly energy generation processes known to the general public. The thought caused Cross to recall the opening line from Alyne's speech he heard not long ago. "Newer, more advanced technologies will naturally replace older, less useful ideas." He wondered about the solar panel he was being sent to examine. Indeed the Skai could have used that technology at less infrastructure expense had the technology been available when Alaka'i was at the drawing board. The Intellagama was a testament to that.

Again, his meandering thoughts brought Cross back to his stint in London less than a year ago and EV3's ARCELOR. The ARCELOR was another clean energy generation device that would best the fuel cell on all accounts, but the world would never know that it existed until it was declassified. Human ambition, thought Cross, had tamed the natural progression for the ARCELOR technology to replace older, less useful ideas. That human ambition may just keep it hidden for some time to come. He couldn't shake the thought.

Cross had spent the last year making sense of the ARCELOR and his entangled escapade with Sirena Raven and EV3's CEO, Nathan Cain. It aggravated him to think that an egomaniacal narcissist like Cain had exclusive control of a technology as profound as the ARCELOR.

Cross was plagued by his awareness of the ARCELOR's incredible power. Its secret was protected by the CENTURI program and its TOP SECRET classification status. Cross wondered what it would have been like today if the ARCELOR technology were made known to the public some 25 years ago when it came into existence? This very vehicle, thought Cross, would have been powered by an ARCELOR had Alaka'i known of the technology when developing the Skai.

Cross imagined an alternate present with another part of his mind; Another now. A reality in which yesterday's truths, hidden from the general populace, had been revealed in a monumental ceremony at the 2012 London Olympics. Ethan was just a toddler then, but he could envision his parents being present at the ARCELOR's unveiling. It would have been a moon-shot event that that generation would look back upon with pride and say, "I remember where I was when the ARCELOR was announced. I remember when humanity's reliance on fossil fuels ceased." Instead, the clean-abundant energy revolution remained underground, hidden from view in the annals of the secretive defense industry. A truth that Ethan and a select few others outside of EV3 now knew.

Evidence of a warming world was gripping the globe everywhere. Cross was frustrated thinking that a technology existed that could at once solve energy constraints on the planet and start to reverse the greenhouse warming that threatened to make places like Dubai unlivable. The stunning view out of his sky-borne taxis' window brought him back to his true present.

The eclectic city skyline passed beyond the expansive windows of Cross' autonomous chariot. Many of the structures towered high above his 500-foot high flight path. The tips of the Burj Khalifa tower and a more modern sky scrapper erected nearby it was another thousand feet above him. The new taller building, now square in his view through the taxis' tinted glass ceiling, was built to best Saudi Arabia's Jeddah Tower height. The more contemporary building had secured the new world record as the world's tallest standing structure. Dubai would not be outdone by the neighboring country. It was more evidence of advancing technology replacing older. Older, in this case, being the fabled Burj Khalifa tower and its once record-setting height. Cross re-entered his daydream.

He wondered what he would say to Cain if they ever chanced to meet again? What would Cain have to say to him? Cross respected the man's brilliance even if he had applied it to sinister pursuits. Cain had carefully built an empire that fortified the ARCELOR's secret, ensuring its true nature wouldn't be discovered by anyone he didn't want to know. Cross had been the only breach in Cain's thirty-year-old phalanx of compartmentalized information. Cross knew Cain hated that Cross was at large with his secret, which gave Cross power. A power that he felt helpless to exercise.

Cross had played out various scenarios of publically announcing EV3's ARCELOR in his mind. He had considered publishing the news, but without verifiable evidence, coming out with a claim of the existence of such revolutionary new technology would sound like sensational fiction. It would be an invitation for another government cover-up, and it might have the opposite effect, leaving the secret of the ARCELOR forever locked away and undisclosed.

And the risk to his stellar, low profile, professional reputation that would come from going to the media with Cain's secret made Cross shutter. Cross shunned the limelight that would surely accompany his leaking of the story. Besides, the technology was still classified by the CENTURI program, and his Top Secret clearance status prohibited him from whistleblowing without severe legal consequences. The prospect of publicity gave Cross pangs of anxiety. It wasn't his style. Cross hated drawing attention to himself and abhorred being publically recognized.

Still, to anonymously leak the ARCELOR's existence was a power Cross had over Cain, and Cain knew it.

Cross wondered what Cain's next play would be? Knowing that someone outside his sphere of control was aware of his secret, what measure would he be willing to take to keep that power from the masses? To date, that answer seemed to be; nothing. The status quo had been undisturbed. There had been no unusual activity in the news that Cross could detect related to EV3. If they were taking steps to further shield the quantum leap in technology from the public, they were careful about it. ARCELOR technology remained controlled by a single corporation run by elite individuals. No different than how fossil fuels controlled by royal family cartels funded the construction of the city racing by below Ethan. Greed kept the ARCELOR hidden for private use. How, Cross wondered, did EV3 hope to keep the ARCELOR secret for another 30 years, and why? For now, the answer seemed to be, wait. Who would make the first move? Cross or Cain? The breach in the dike was holding even if Cain couldn't control when or if Cross would choose to remove his finger from the one hole in the dam. Cross shook the daydream and turned his attention to his latest source of intrigue: A rocket fairing laced with a solar panel found at sea.

He reflected on his recent message from Logan Kraft the night before. The email had indicated that the fairing recovered from the ocean was of Chinese origin. Furthermore, the leading hypothesis was that it came from a payload launched by Rocket Sci in New Zealand.

It was a small world, thought Cross, for him to have chanced to meet someone from the company on the same day that Logan had put him onto a new assignment with which Rocket Sci may be involved. Cross would have liked to ask Alyne what she knew about it. He would have liked to have said goodbye. He would have liked to see her again. Such was his challenge with meeting a girl worthy of his time. He had high standards in pursuit of a girlfriend. The frequent travel demands of his job made it difficult to get to know anyone. Familiarity breeds relationship, and he found that he rarely had enough time to become familiar, let alone trust, anyone as a partner. He struck a memory of deceit from his mind.

His relationship with Ila Roane, whom he had spent some time with after London, was one exception. Sadly, that relationship had fallen victim to a mutual separation in geography. They both knew the valence of their professions would keep them apart; still, she was good about keeping Cross on the distribution of a monthly astrology horoscope she published. A routine periodical that Cross had come to find mildly amusing. It had become a guilty pleasure of Cross' to read the few paragraphs she would send. He would read with fascination and disbelief that some people believed that the motion of the planets and stars could have any bearing on events in their lives.

Cross preferred the exactness of science and engineering to the subjective and mystical nature of things like horoscopes. He felt a better partner would be rational and scientific, someone like Alyne Jimmie. He remembered his feelings for another brilliant woman, a beautiful siren who had been logical and calculating; Sirena Raven. Cross didn't have the same closure with her. That relationship had ended abruptly, for good reason, but something about it felt undone.

Nonetheless, his experience teaming with Sirena

made it hard for Cross to trust a partner, be it a coworker or otherwise. It was just as well; he liked to work alone. His fuel-cell-powered air taxi neared the Dubai International Airport.

Cross fired up his comm-specs with a touch of an ear stay button and began to research his ultimate destination. The Ronald Reagan Ballistic Missile Defense test site on Kwajalein atoll. It was thousands of miles ahead of him, a few connecting flights away, and dozens of in-flight pretzel bags from Dubai. No supersonic flights operated there. Cross would have plenty of time to research the location just a few hundred miles from the Bikini islands, where the United States had tested another device of great power over 100 years ago, the Atomic Bomb.

| Chapter 5 |

Sea Gull

Kwajalein. Marshall Islands

The small commercial jet buffeted in the central Pacific wind as it descended to the remote atoll. Cross had been in the air for just over three hours since his latest flight had taken off from Guam. It was the last leg in an arduous series of transfers on his way from Dubai. His window seat was toward the back of the jet, and from the tiny portal, he could see that the vehicle was approaching what looked like a miss-shapen ring of the white caps of waves. The plane continued its descent. As they approached the Pacific Ocean's surface, Cross realized that what he had thought were waves a moment before were tiny strips of land. His destination was a series of small islands that from above seemed to resemble the outline of the state of Florida traced by a six-year-old kid on a sugar rush. Cross had looked up his destination in his comm-specs along the way and learned that it is one of the world's largest coral atolls- as measured by the area of water enclosed by the 97 small islands and islets situated along its perimeter. Kwajalein Island is the southernmost and largest island in the atoll, after which it is named. Cross moved to the edge of his passenger seat to get a better view. The island itself was boomerang-shaped, and the airstrip spanned the entire distance of the bend. Giving the six square mile strip of sand credit as the largest island was like receiving the most improved player award in grade school gym class. One day, maybe you'll be a real island, thought Cross. His plane turned onto its final approach. As the jet banked out of its base leg, the tiny runway pivoted to the aircraft's nose, away from Cross' view. He imagined being in the pilot's seat and wondered how different the landing was from lining up with an aircraft carrier's deck. Cross thought, *I hope he's done this before. We are about to land on a postage stamp!*

The plane came to a stop before the end of the runway without the splash into the Pacific that had played out in Cross' minds-eye. Cross unbuckled his seat belt with relief. He had traveled 1,500 miles from Guam. Cross couldn't imagine a place more remote. He was 2,100 miles southwest of Honolulu, 2,100 miles east of Japan, and 2,000 miles northeast of Australia. The equator was 500 miles south, but it wasn't like the equator was a landmark Cross could visit for a burger. Kwajalein was in the geographic middle of nowhere. It was a nowhere of significant strategic military importance, however.

In World War II, the US Navy hosted a naval base on Kwajalein before transferring operational control to the US Army Kwajalein Atoll, or USAKA. For just under one hundred years now, the US Army has operated the base, initially as part of their Nike Zeus anti-ballistic missile efforts. Since then, the atoll has been widely used for missile tests of all sorts. Kwajalein most famously served as the staging location for 23 nuclear bomb tests by the United States, detonated just 200 miles northwest in the Bikini Islands. Almost one hundred years ago, Bikini atoll's inhabitants were relocated to Kwajalein before the US government destroyed their pristine Marshall Islands homes with a series of atomic bomb tests. Many descendants of those relocated Marshallese remain on Ebeye, a small islet north of the eastern end of Kwajalein Island, which used to be accessible by foot at low tide when ocean levels were lower.

Today, Kwajalein is part of the USAKA Ronald Reagan Ballistic Missile Defense Test Site, with radars, missile launchers, and many support systems spread across multiple islands. It is a missile test range positioned at the heart of the Pacific that primarily functions as a test facility for U.S. missile defense and space research programs operating a series of strategic radar tracking assets.

Doctor David Archie Dodge worked for MIT Lincoln Laboratory services. He was part of a team of civilian SETA contractors deployed there as the scientific advisors to the Reagan Test Site at the USAKA installation. Doctor Dodge's primary function was to support upgrades to the command-and-control and Radar infrastructure of the range. He designed many of his own real-time discrimination algorithms, a vocation he had worked diligently at for most of his career, but the man also had hobbies. He had elected to remain stationed at Kwaj longer than most. He was approaching a record-breaking 25-year service milestone at the remote station. Dr.

Dodge wore his island life isolation like a favorite Hawaiian shirt. His unshaven grey beard, sandals, and untucked shirt projected a Jimmie Buffet first impression before the radio systems Ph.D. Cross knew Dodge to be. Cross pushed his comm-specs up onto his forehead as Doctor Dodge approached him across the facility's otherwise vacant reception area. The man moved slowly and had a slight hunch back. He walked like he needed a cane, but he had none.

"Archie Dodge." He stuck out his hand with a friendly greeting. He didn't ask or give Cross a chance to offer his name, "So you're Logan's man? No doubt he told you we found it floating in the ocean a couple of weeks ago during a night sail. We still have many questions, but it appears to be part of a rocket's nose cone. It's a curious specimen for several reasons. First of all, it's got solar panels embedded in its surface. Now that wouldn't be too perplexing if it weren't for the fact that the panel is installed on the interior."

Cross had a fleeting acknowledgment that his host had skipped the glad-handing and small talk that usually accompanied an introductory greeting. Instead, Doctor Dodge had dove into the matter at hand, facts first. Cross liked that. Dodge was his kind of guy.

"Yes. Logan mentioned the inner surface was a solar panel." Cross repeated.

"We can't figure out what purpose that would serve. One side has a control flap, like an airplane wing's trailing edge. We figure that it must guide it to some unknown recovery point. It's also got an electronics box at the base of it. We haven't been able to assess its purpose fully. We've identified part of the circuitry and some of the code as a guidance, navigation, and control unit...which is why you're here...deciphering that part needs an expert. The other parts of the circuitry are recognizable as a power rectifier."

Wow, by way of an introduction, that was a mouthful. Cross was interested in that last part. "A power rectifier? You mean circuitry to change alternating current to direct current, like in the transformers of pretty much every piece of consumer electronics you plug in at home?" He tapped his comm-specs and repositioned them on his brow, remembering that they were good for a few days before a charge. They couldn't transmit to satellites; they only received, which helped with power consumption. Cross was eager to view the enigmatic piece of rocket hardware Dodge was describing in person.

"Correct, but it seems to capture the energy at a very high frequency. The alternating signals, or the sine waves it can receive, are very small. We're talking nanometers, as in a billion would fit into a meter."

"That is impressive."

"Impressive? How about incredible? You probably have a decent grasp of how big a centimeter is. Remember that 10 millimeters fit into one centimeter, so millimeters are already pretty small. Now listen to this: there are one MILLION nanometers in just one millimeter!"

"Ok, I get it, it's wicked small," Cross' Boston came out.

"Yeah, small is an understatement. I've never seen manufacturing on a scale this small. Each tiny antenna is roughly 1 micron or 1/10,000,000th of a meter long and made from a carbon nanotube. An ultra-fast diode at one end of the antenna can operate at frequencies approaching one picohertz. That's one quadrillion cycles per second." The Doctor paused for emphasis. "Each one is connected to rectifying circuitry that converts that alternating current into usable direct current." Dodge watched his guest for an acknowledgment of the extreme engineering feat. Cross nodded. Dodge continued. "By contrast, short wave radios operate at frequencies in low megahertz or roughly a million cycles per second. For FM and AM radio antennas, the antenna needs to be roughly a meter long like those in your car. The difference is a factor of one billion." Archie waited for Cross to react.

"So antennae are sized for the wavelengths they are designed to receive?"

"That's right." Confirmed Dodge.

"And the device is converting sunlight into energy as an ordinary solar cell does, just by a different process?"

"Yes. This panel can convert weak light to small amounts of power. I estimate this one puts out three or four times the energy for the same exposure to sunlight as an equivalent-sized traditional photovoltaic solar cell. There are roughly one trillion tiny radio receivers per square inch. They likely operate over a broader range of frequencies from low infrared through visible light and up into the ultraviolet."

"A trillion? Wow, may I see it?"

"Of course, of course, I thought you'd never ask. I'll take you to my tinkering station on the Lagoon. The fairing is there laid out on my workbench near the schooner. It's become a hot curiosity here, you know. I hate the thought of losing it into the ether of bureaucracy before we crack the mystery. You're about a day, maybe a day and a half ahead of the MISC officials or the Aussies from Alice Springs, not certain who will arrive first. That's why I called Logan- for answers. It would be a most unsatisfying end to the most stimulating thing that's washed up here in ages." Archie gave another hermit snicker.

"Washed up here? How did you find it again?"

"Figure of speech. It didn't wash up. We found it a few hundred miles south of here, just floating at sea while we were tooling around in the schooner one night a few weekends ago."

"You found it floating in the open ocean? What are

the chances of that?" Ethan inquired with surprise.

"Well, it stuck out like a lighthouse; at first, we thought it was a small boat on the horizon."

"You could see it on the horizon? Didn't you say you were sailing at night?"

Archie snickered again, clearly aware of something that he hadn't shared. Cross felt like Skywalker must have during his first encounter with Yoda on Dagobah. Archie was dodging something obvious.

"I think it's better if I just show you. Follow me this way." The old salt waddled his way out of the facility exit with a shuffle to his step. He moved sideways like a sand crab, reaching out to nearby furniture for support as he moved along. Cross thought to himself. *Follow me this way? I'll just walk as I usually do.*

Doctor Dodge led Cross into the parking lot like a Quasimodo energizer bunny. They approached a faded old golf cart decorated with a front grille, like a Jeep. It had no doors and no roof. Cross thought that this vehicle must have been as old as Dodge himself. He sat back in the antique.

"She's a beaut, ain't she? There are no real cars allowed on Kwaj. Everyone gets around in these buggies. I picked her up when I first moved here 25 short years ago. She was new then. That was before she earned her reputation as the Jeep-Kart," Archie spoke as he piloted the vehicle toward the inner shore of the island. "She made the trek over to Ebeye once at low tide. Some Marshallese youths took her for a joy ride across the land bridge. Because of the rising ocean levels, it remained over there for some time until one lucky day that the water receded enough, and I got permission from the base commander to drive her back at low tide again. It was rough going, but she made it," Dodge slapped the steering wheel, "That's when I made her a new grill, and she's been the Jeep-Kart ever since."

They approached the marina. Archie parked the Jeep-Kart relic and led the way out onto Echo pier. Ethan looked around for a sailboat, but he saw none, let alone a sizable one that could be referred to as a schooner. They approached a run-down boathouse with utilitarian metal siding and an aluminum roof. It looked more like an aircraft hanger than a boathouse. It was a low single-story structure that hung from the pier over the water. Cross gauged it to be nearly as old as their Jeep-Kart chariot. Was nothing on this island new? Cross watched Archie key a few digits on a mechanical cipher lock. He could see that each button Dodge depressed was worn from years of use, 1-8-3-6. Dodge commented on the worn cipher lock as the mechanism released, granting them access to the boathouse. "It's no Vigenere encryption, but it's enough to deter the occasional Marshallese adolescent from wandering in and causing mischief." The hanger door closed behind them.

Cross thought the building seemed a little too low to accommodate a sailboat's mast. Archie spoke as he revealed the view like a magician.

"TaDa" He flipped on ancient mercury floodlights. They came on in two sets, illuminating the vacant hanger with audible thuds from closing mechanical relays. Like birthday cake candles lit in rows leading away from the purveyor and his guest, the room got progressively brighter. The threshold where they stood deposited them onto a gangway above the water level. A stealthy, angular-looking ship rode low in the water in front of them.

"Where is the......What is that?" Cross senses had been stunned by the sight of the craft and the missing schooner, like when one is anticipating a cold sip of ice tea but takes a large gulp of carbonated soda instead. Cross repositioned his comm-specs on his forehead for a clearer view, ensuring the shades didn't obscure his vision.

"That's my schooner," Archie said proudly, presenting his punch line with an open arm extended toward the vessel.

"What... is it? It looks like a spacecraft." The ship, if you could call it a ship, rested on its belly but seemed to be meant to float on two pylons like a catamaran. Cross could see a long tubular pod structure that extended the boat's length was submerged below the waterline at the end of each pylon. The exposed hull was a sharp trapezoidal shape. It looked more like an imperial shuttle from Star Wars than a boat. What was Yoda showing him? With a bridge of highly sloped tinted windows that met at a point on the nose of the bow, the water craft looked like it was from the future.

"Aww, this old thing? She's a relic like my old Jeep-Kart out there, only she's got another fifteen years or so on the Jeep."

"That's 40 years old." Cross offered the output of his public math as a statement, even though it was still a question in his head.

"She's one of a kind. The Navy calls it a swath. The hull rides above the waves while the engines are mounted below the surface on these wide blades that cut through the surf. The Army assumed custody of her when the Navy rejected Romeo Marine's final bid for the Ghost interceptor concept over 20 years ago. We got the Ghost here at Kwaj as Government Furnished Equipment to execute a proposal we won to enhance our early warning surface radar ability. Its angular hull and high speed make it ideal for radar cross-section target practice for our detection algorithms. Basic, direct line of sight Radar at sea level can see no further than a person staring at the horizon about 3 miles out, but elevate the transceiver and apply some clever techniques, and one can detect ships like the Ghost far beyond that. After that program fizzled out, no one wanted to pay to move her elsewhere. Over the years, we've successfully got some limited Internal Research and Development (IRAD) funds to upgrade her avionics. We put a forward-looking infrared (FLIR) on her a few years ago.

"The Ghost? What was her original purpose?" Cross proceeded around the gangway to gain more perspective on the craft.

"She was envisioned to help counter the swarm threat to large naval vessels. The Navy wanted something fast and maneuverable to engage cigarette boats ingressing destroyers and carriers. And then, like other gov't contracts, they wanted it to support long-range reconnaissance missions too. With the Ghost ship, the theory of operation was that you could get into denied-access ocean areas and loiter for up to 30 days with the fuel onboard. One could listen to cell phone conversations, monitor what's going on, launch operations and leave, and no one knows you're there. That was the concept, at least. They never quite figured out how to get it to steer properly, so they couldn't meet the original maneuverability requirement....but it is fast!"

"How fast?" asked Cross.

"Upwards of 70 knots. The supercavitation propulsion method used to propel the Ghost is the same that enabled the old Russian Shkval torpedo to gain a speed four times higher than its western counterparts at the beginning of the century. The craft is designed so that the main hull lifts above water when the Ghost moves at speeds over eight knots. Its original powerplants were two T53-703 turboshaft engines seated in pontoons. We've had those upgraded, of course, but the concept remains the same. The engines power a counter-rotating propeller located at the front of each pod. The propellers create a 'supercavitation' effect, enabling the pod to carry the entire vessel on a bubble trail rather than through the denser sea-water, thus achieving 900 times less hull friction."

"And what is the antenna on the top?" Ethan turned his attention to four antennas spaced equidistant from each other on the roof of the ghost in a square arrangement. The leading two stood slightly shorter than the rear two, but only by a foot or two, mounted on a lower cabin roof area. All four seemed to be telescoped down into a stowed position.

"Those are my schooner masts. They reach close to one hundred feet tall when fully extended outside the hanger. A true schooner is differentiated from a multi-mast sailboat whose bow mast is lower than its stern. The Ghost is my schooner...and I'm a HAM."

"Logan said you were a Ham." Ethan didn't think it was all that funny.

"Logan used that old pun on you, did he? He's overused that trite bit of humor since he and I dormed together at the institute. Haha."

Ethan had missed the joke, "What pun are you referring to?" Usually, Cross prided himself on his ability to pick up on puns or crack them himself.

"I'm an Amateur radio enthusiast. A HAM. I'm not

sure what Logan told you, but if he said that old Archie Dodge is a real HAM...well, that's a joke he's been using for years."

"Yes, that's exactly what he said" Ethan understood the HAM reference now.

"The actual meaning of HAM is taken from the three pioneers that helped make it possible for all of us to become "HAMS." As a teacher, Doctor Dodge began a lesson.

"The letter H stands for Hertz, Heinrich Hertz, who helped develop the theory of electromagnetic waves.

The letter A stands for Armstrong, Edwin Howard Armstrong, who successfully invented Frequency Modulation.

As you may have guessed, the letter M stands for Marconi, Gugliemo Marconi, who was the first to transmit signals across the Atlantic without using cables." Dodge hobbled a few shuffles to another vantage point and pointed at the water craft's roof.

"The schooners masts are an array of four antenna's installed in a square arrangement like that which is useful for interferometry of all the signals in the shortwave frequency band when fully extended. Each one is about one quarter the wavelength of shortwave radio waves."

"Interferometry?" Ethan was familiar with spectrometry for measuring wavelengths of light, but Interferometry?

"Yes, direction-finding. I can use that array on top to locate the angle of arrival of an incoming signal and use it as a barring. It's especially effective when the schooner is on the move." Dodge motioned to a map on the wall.

Ethan saw a giant Pacific-centered map of the globe mounted above Archie's workstation. It was a giant version of the map on the face of Cross' wristwatch. Cross was impressed by the size of the cartograph. It was unique to see the world projected that way, with Australia in the center surrounded by the continents. It felt much more balanced than the maps to which he was accustomed. It was a refreshing perspective to see someplace other than the United States centered on the globe. The Mercator projection had pins in nearly every country. On the desk below was what looked to be an open logbook. It had fields with titles such as the date, frequency, mode and power output, contact station name and location, call sign and Zulu time. "What is all this?" Cross motioned to both the map and the logbook.

"That's my HAM log. HAM radio signals can travel for thousands and thousands of miles across the world, some of them. Those are all the places I've made HAM contacts. I've reached someone in nearly every country. I'm working on the Pacific islands now." He gestured to the wall nearby, adorned with medals, trophies, and certificates. Some of the awards were printed on paper.

They were faded with many years of age and from exposure to the Pacific's salty air. "Still trying to reach someone at Pitcairn, VP6PAC- 1836 KHz. It's one of the few places I need to reach, but I'm afraid it's gone silent key."

"You reach people from all over the globe from right here with this old radio equipment?" Cross was intrigued that such old equipment could accomplish the feat.

"Oh yeah. And from onboard the Ghost." He pointed to the quad antenna array on the roof. "It's old tech. It has been around for a couple of hundred years now unlike frequencies used by FM radio stations, TV stations, and by aircraft and marine communications, which are line-of-sight and therefore limited to 40 or 50 miles, short-waves "bounce" off the ionosphere from the transmitter to the receiver's antenna. HAM signals can even bounce off the moon! This old Sea Gull may have a world record for all the places where I've confirmed contacts," Archie laughed proudly. "Sea Gull, it's my HAM handle."

"Your handle, like a pilot call sign? How'd you choose that name?" Ethan thought it was an appropriate choice for an old salt castaway on a reef like a lighthouse operator in the middle of the ocean.

"The Sea Gull was another fine schooner." He looked back at the Ghost with a paternal smile. "The Sea Gull was part of the United States first exploration mission of the Pacific Islands in 1836." Cross gave him some leeway.

Pontificating was a side effect of prolonged isolation. Dodge was interesting; nonetheless, "The Sea Gull went silent key too. It was lost at sea, attempting to return by Cape Horn. There's a monument in the Mount Auburn Cemetery in Cambridge, Massachusetts, for her, you know. Not far from my Alma Mata. It lists the officers who were lost on the Sea Gull surveying uncharted Pacific Islands."

"Silent Key?" Ethan had heard the Doctor say it twice now. He knew the term Key was another word for island, and he reasoned the meaning had to do with that. "Do you mean Hidden Island?" Cross surmised.

"No. Silent Key. It's the term HAM's use when a station operator passes away. I suppose it's a coincidence now that the date of the Sea Gull's faithful exploration expedition of the Polynesia triangle in 1836 shares the same frequency as my elusive quarry. 1836 kHz- VP6PAC, that's Pitcairn's HAM station frequency," Ethan noted the curious coincidence.

"1836 kHz," Cross echoed as he watched Dodge shuffle across the hanger to the work station below the world.

Dodge finally reached the map, supporting himself on the desk at Cross' side. He pointed at an island. "Tahiti. Now that's a Pacific Island where I'd like to get lost at sea. I want to sail my schooner there before the upcoming solar eclipse. Maybe retire there. Bora Bora seems like a place for an old islander like me to scuttle his schooner and disappear." Doctor Dodge trailed off before he changed the subject back to HAM. "The hobby has become less and less popular in recent years. HAM is becoming a lost art due to the prevalence of the internet."

"Yes, it seems like every major company has their own constellation of internet satellites these days." Ethan thought of Rick Chan's description of Solcom's space-based internet satellites.

"Oh yes, but that's not how most data on the internet is exchanged around the world."

"It's not? It seems like that's all you hear about lately. Kuiper, Starlink, even Solcom, an up and coming Chinese company, has a Low Earth Orbit network called Icarus." Offered Cross.

"Naw. Those satellite constellations service only a small fraction of the data exchanged, and they are only good for fast download speeds. The upload speed to low earth-orbiting satellites from a small low powered mobile device like a comm-band or a comm-spec is abysmal at best. The real backbone of the internet is undersea cables. We have a major fiber-optic artery feeding Kwajalein, in fact. It comes from Guam. Thank god, else we'd be pretty isolated here." Archie laughed again. Ethan laughed with the man and at his ironic statement. Dodge displayed the eccentric tendencies that prolonged isolation must cause.

"The reality is only a small volume of international

telecommunications is delivered via satellite. Take Australia, for instance; a limited number of undersea cable services 95 to 99 percent of Australia's internet need. Mostly they feed into Sydney and Perth. I think one may feed into Brisbane, but the country has had notoriously slow internet access among the developed nations for years."

"I didn't know that. Interesting, I never gave it much thought, I guess. Who pays for running cables across whole oceans?"

"Oh yeah, undersea cables are big business. Governments fund the projects and major companies you wouldn't necessarily associate with significant infrastructure projects. The private industry has invested millions in establishing and maintaining the network. It's been going on since as far back as 1858, a few decades before Marconi aimed the first radio signals at North America from England, the US and the UK collaborated on the first transatlantic telegraph cable. It reduced the communication time between North America and Europe from ten days—the time it took to deliver a message by ship—to a matter of minutes. Internet companies like Google and Facebook have financed new cable runs to Asia and elsewhere for the last few decades. It doesn't get as much press as Satellites because it's less sexy. Being better has its place. Newer, more advanced technologies will naturally replace older, less useful ideas. Satellites are the new sexy way to get information from point A to point B, but they'll never outdo a couple of hundred years of tried and true cable laying." It was a thought-provoking perspective. It made Ethan think of a similar thought he had leaving Dubai about the flying boat's evolution from the Sikorsky's S-38 to MagiX's Intelagama. One hundred years later, and flying boats still have utility. Despite the new sexy technology it possessed, the Intelagama was a variation on an old proven concept. Fascinating, thought Cross, that undersea cables, not satellites, were the internet's backbone. Doctor Dodge switched his attention to the reason they were here.

"Speaking of sexy, here's the fairing." Doctor Dodge started into an orientation of all that he had accomplished and discovered about the fairing. He explained how the fairing appeared white in the Ghost ship's infrared display as it floated on the ocean waves. He showed Cross where he had tapped into the circuitry and how he had figured out how to gain access to the firmware.

"Would you like some help deciphering the code?" He pulled up the text file reader on the screen. "I'm no programmer, but I understood some of it. Not enough, I'm afraid, which is why I called Logan, and why you're here, of course."

"I prefer to work alone," Cross said flatly as he stepped toward the artifact that had drawn him across the planet.

| Chapter 6 |

Coordinates

"You don't have much time. We could have visitors in a couple of days. If you can find out anything more before the authorities confiscate it, I'd be in your debt."

Cross nodded, eager to delve into his work without interruption.

"I'll leave you to it then. The Jeep-Kart is yours for the night. The keys are in it. I'm going to walk on over to the American Eatery. Would you like anything?"

"No, thank you," Ethan said, eager to get started.

"Very well, suit yourself. Let's catch up in the morning. I'm interested to hear what you find."

Cross settled in at the well-used HAM operator station. In front of him lay his quarry. It extended the length of the workbench. The intricate rocket fairing exuded value. It wasn't the exotic material alone that drove the impression. It was the tight tolerances apparent in its construction. It was a fine piece of craftsmanship. The slight curl of its shape was reminiscent of a modern windmill blade. An aileron flight control surface was formed into what appeared to Cross to be the trailing edge. He inspected it closer. Along what he figured was the bottom, he traced his fingers along a rib that seemed to have the counter contour of the fairings leading edge. Yes. When installed on the nose of a rocket, the flap appeared to tuck behind the edge of the adjacent fairing. Cross could envision the ingenious assembly; each aileron stowed away from view until the whole mechanism was released like a giant Fabergé egg.

Cross turned his attention to the root of the wing. A cover panel had been removed from an electronics box at the base of its twisted shape—the seamlessly integrated mold line showed evidence of Doctor Dodge's struggle to gain entry. He had gained access using crude tools, but he had been careful with his surgery after that. The exposed electronics had been kept clean. A makeshift cable ran from a test port to the workstation's computer. The terminal was positioned where Cross could navigate the code displayed on the screen while peering into the foreign circuitry.

The Doctor had pioneered a rudimentary yet capable set of diagnostic tools. A pair of old-school dual flat-screen Liquid Crystal Display monitors was at his disposal. Of course, Cross thought, Archie, the man who piloted a 25-year-old Jeep-Kart and a half-century-old relic of defense technology gone by, wouldn't be set up with a modern workstation with the requisite glass board display panels and laser keyboard to which Cross was accustomed.

Cross sat and dove into reviewing the code on the right-hand monitor being piped to the archaic display panel from the hardware on the operating table in front of him. He read from the top down. Chinese characters that he didn't understand appeared periodically, but the conditional function structure was familiar. He recognized the matrix math. He scanned over direction cosine matrices and a mixture of Euler operands and quaternion calculations. After a few minutes of scrolling the screen, something caught his eye. He recognized all of it as the guidance portion of the algorithm, but where was the code guiding the unit? There, he saw it; A comparator function.

The hardware's current location was supplied to the code from an embedded global positioning system receiver with integrated attitude sensors. That was well-established technology. Cross wasn't interested in that. He wanted to know the final position to which the comparator function matched the current location. He was looking for something that would look like a coordinate. He knew that the navigation code would be designed to calculate how far the device was from some predetermined destination by subtracting where it was from where it needed to be. The code would work to minimize the distance between the two. That simple arithmetic would be the engine behind the complex translation of that knowledge into the control surface inputs needed to steer the unit as it spun to its ultimate destination. Something must have gone awry with the communication to the aileron. Cross correctly figured that the arrival point would be unaffected by whatever malfunction plagued the ill-fated journey. Yes. There it was, Cross spotted a constant that looked like a line of Latitude and Longitude. It read:

20° 8' 29" S, 158° 37' 4"E (-20.14159, 158.61803)

He jotted the coordinates down on a nearby yellow sticky note:

Latitude 20 degrees, 8 minutes, 29 seconds South, Longitude 158 degrees, 37 minutes, 4 seconds East.

He took a moment to reach up to his comm-specs and slid them down over his eyes. He depressed a small button that he knew from the feel of its shape to his fingertips. He snapped a photo of the coordinates along with a fragment of the code displayed on the screen.

Cross hastily entered the coordinates into a map search on the left-hand monitor. The map panned a few thousand miles southwest of his location at Kwajalein to a solid blue position in the middle of the open water North East of Australia. He zoomed out—the Coral Sea. Nothing was there but an expanse of blue ocean. He must have transcribed the coordinates incorrectly. He added the text 'The Coral Sea' to the sticky note and stuck it onto Dodge's old terminal monitor. He'd come back to that.

Cross continued this study of the algorithm. He scrolled down. Another few minutes passed. His eyelids felt heavy, but he forced his eyes to open wider.

A conditional statement passed his field of view from the bottom to the screen's top. He stopped the scroller and moved the screen back to take a closer look. The line of code called a function that Cross recognized to reference the time of day. It was a fork in the road of the computer code that told the electronics to do something different at a specific time. It was logic based on a clock. The behavior of the device would change between two specified times. He read the times bounding a conditional statement, 17:56 UTC+11 Apparent Sunset and 0531 UTC+11 Apparent Sunrise. The first time corresponded to sunset in Oceania, the timezone of the coordinates Cross had noted elsewhere in the code. After the specified time, the algorithm began to look different. No longer was code commanding the electronics to generate power from sunlight. Instead, the code looked more like a radio receiver. Yes. He scrolled on. He recognized digital signal processing algorithms.

He turned his head to look at the hardware on the desk. Another section of the electronics to the test cable's right was still covered. It was a smaller portion of the circuit card assembly than the real estate devoted to the power conditioning electronics. Cross scanned the workbench for a screwdriver. He reached into the assembly and gently pried back the cover of the undisturbed portion. The interior lid yielded readily to the leverage. Cross leaned in to remove the cover. He saw what he knew to be a digital receiver under the protective cover. He knew Doctor Dodge would recognize it too.

It was getting late. Cross could feel the weight of his eyelids pulling at his attention. He shook it off. It had been a long series of fights to reach Kwajalein since

Dubai. He was fueled by anticipation. There was so much more code to review. He wondered what else he could glean about the enigmatic rocket hardware. He was eager to share what he had already found with Doctor Dodge. He wanted more answers than questions before reporting back to Logan Kraft. He forced himself to focus. The lines of code were running together. Perhaps he could shut his eyes for a moment, just to clear his mind. Yes, he'd rest his head for a few minutes and go at it again with a fresh start. He put his forehead on his forearm on the desktop in front of the terminal. Cross dozed off into a deep slumber.

| Chapter 7 |

Shadow on the Sun

EV3 Headquarters, Chelmsford. England.

"What we need is a cloak. A shield. A mirage." Nathan Cain addressed the assembly of stakeholders in the EV3 second-story conference room. His voice boomed through the phone to the employee who had called into the meeting. "For the first time in over three decades, the true nature of the ARCELOR is known to someone outside of our organization. We are at a juncture." Cain stood from his seat at the head of the long board room table. He referred to Ethan Cross without speaking his name. The CEO walked to face the wall of windows that overlooked the company's half-length football field. Cain spoke again as he gazed through the glass. "Over three decades ago, the universe presented a problem at the same time it revealed a solution. The ARCELOR; It is our responsibility to the human race to bring the ARCELOR to bear on this problem. We are faced with the unfavorable prospect of enacting our long-term plans far earlier than we anticipated, lest we find a shroud for the ARCELOR, a veil to protect her from prying eyes. Long have I pondered on this dilemma. How do we keep the ARCELOR hidden in plain sight from the world while we continue our work?" Cain turned away from the window to face the room of captive participants.

He focused on the modern saucer-shaped phone

sitting on the table. It cast an eerie frozen three-dimensional profile image of a beautiful woman with jet black hair above the table's surface. The woman was calling into the affair from abroad. She was dialed in from across the globe via a stylish pair of mobile comm-specs. As was common with comm-spec connections from remote locations where only satellite internet connections were available, her video feed was one way. She could view the room of board members on the inside of her glasses, but a video of her likeness could not be streamed to the room due to both the upload bandwidth limitation of the satellite network, which was just as well to Sirena because she sat reclined on the lounge chair on the private top pool deck. No camera was set up to view her flawless face. Instead, her pre-recorded avatar mug shot hovered in the center of the table projected from a holographic prism for all to see. It was a familiar apparition to attendees of the monthly recurring meeting as she had been operating as an Expat for over a year since leaving Portsmouth harbor aboard one EV3's Panacea cruise ships bound for the South Pacific after a call in Miami. Cain continued to address the attendees.

"The ARCELOR is the heart of a star. Our Star. It's the centerpiece of our enterprise. It's the core of EV3's empire. It's the key to humanity's future. For many months now, we've convened to discuss ideas to protect her, to keep her under lock and key, to maintain the Crown's greatest state secret. To date, I've heard no viable options from any of you." He shot a disapproving glance at his Chief Technical Officer, Alan Fortinbras. He carried on, "Again, are there any new ideas to direct attention away from her until we decide her secret can be revealed? I need something- anything that would cast a shadow of doubt on her true nature?" Cain's frustration was familiar to the participants.

The room was silent. Miss Sirena Raven spoke through the phone.

"I may have something." Her English accent broadcast clearly to all the EV3 board members. He knew that she would continue without encouragement. Still, Cain prompted her to elaborate. She was one of the few EV3 employees to which Cain afforded some autonomy.

"Please proceed. It's about time we've had a fresh idea on this topic, a viable one." He glared at Fortinbras as he granted Sirena leeway to take control of the discussion via the phone. After his latest failed concept, Fortinbras dared not offer another half-conceived notion, which he had shared at another session. Fortinbras had voiced a plan for a smear campaign of Ethan Cross to discredit any public claim he may make about the ARCELOR. Cain had promptly pointed out that Fortinbras' idea assumed Cross would make the first move. The strategy was reactive and did nothing to prevent the very situation they sought to avoid. Cain had shut Fortinbras' idea down, signaling that he would tolerate only pro-active strategies.

"Have you heard of the Intellagama?" Sirena paused for emphasis while she sipped a green umbrella drink only she could see. No one responded. "It's an amphibious electric commuter jet. It recently earned worldwide notoriety for nearly circumnavigating the globe here in the southern hemisphere."

"What's unique about that?" Cain countered. "Many aircraft boast the ability to fly around the world."

"It did so in a single day. Or, to be more accurate, it took off at sunrise and landed at sunset back here in Sydney, never crossing into darkness. The Intellagama generates all the electricity its engines need using a unique new solar cell technology from another company here in Australia named NoviX. Their stock has soared ever since but has seen a significant decline in recent days."

Cain's mind processed the gravity of her statement. Then he smiled. He pointed his smiling face at his chief technology officer. Alan Fortinbras caught on and smiled back, hoping for his superior's approval. Cain's chief of security sat by the conference room entrance. The mountain of a man watched the two men smiling and smiled to mimic them, revealing a missing front tooth. Dante didn't understand what the business leaders had realized. Cain responded slowly.

"Smells like time for a hostile takeover."

"I already have a man on the inside on our payroll." Sirena offered.

"NoviX. I like it." He paused pensively. "Miss Raven, I think you may have found just the thing to cast a shadow on our sun."

| Chapter 8 |

Silent Key

Kwajalein. Marshall Islands

Cross awoke with a start. A hand on his shoulder and a deep voice interrupted the fathoms of his Rapid Eye Movement sleep.

"We'll take it from here, son." A man in a black suit and tie wearing dark comm-spec sunglasses spoke to him. Cross sat up straight as the man, and a clone of the man standing beside the first came into focus. Behind the two twin-shaded men, Archie Dodge stood, waiting.

"Clarence Jones, Missile Space Intelligence Center." The serious Alabamian said with finality. "We've got this now," Jones helped Cross out of the chair to his feet.

Cross stepped over to Doctor Dodge. Dodge leaned in and spoke in a whisper as Cross rubbed his eyes.

"They touched down less than an hour ago and insisted I take them straight here to see the fairing. It looks like these good-old MISC boys from 'Bama beat the Alice Springs folks to the punch. It's just as well. The USAKA base here on Kwaj is theirs anyway."

The Doctor and Cross watched the men hastily package up the rocket shell fragment.

"I told them everything I learned. The MISC men didn't offer much, but they did confirm that it's from a rocket launched a few weeks ago from Aurhihi Point in New Zealand."

"Where can we reach Logan Kraft from? Do you have a secure line?"

"I've got a STE phone back at the office. I've already sent him an unclassified message to arrange a call time."

Cross followed Archie out of the hanger, glancing back at the desk where the men from MSIC were confiscating the aeroshell. Cross stole a final gaze at Ghost Ship that sat low in the boathouse. The site of the antennas configured for radio frequency direction finding, staggered on its roof like masts of a schooner, reminded Cross of the Doctor's story of the Sea Gull that had been lost at sea. They would have no more opportunity to study the curious rocket solar panel. Like Dodge's lost Pacific island of Pitcairn, the fairing had gone silent key.

The two men sat together in front of the Secure Terminal Equipment land-line phone. The STE was developed in the early 1990s by the National Security Agency for crypto communications for the United States government, its contractors, and allies. Like everything on Kwajalein, it was a relic. Cross was amazed it was still in commission. Then again, he had learned that the Secure Telephone Unit, or STU phone, the STE's predecessor remained in commission for nearly 40 years from 1960. It was quickly phased out due to the operational difficulties that hindered coordination between the Federal Aviation Administration and NORAD during the September 11, 2001 attacks on New York and Washington almost 50 years ago. Like Archie himself, this antique STE may be the last of its kind, thought Cross.

Dodge put a worn PC card containing cryptographic algorithms into a slot in the STE at the specified time. The ancient machinery recognized the Fortezza Plus Crypto Card he inserted. Dodge picked up the handset and dialed the telephone number using the STE keypad. It was an archaic process, but Archie commented under his breath, suggesting that he considered the encryption technique to be modern. "Beats using a Tabula Recta...." Cross smiled in silence, uncertain of the reference. Logan was waiting in a Secure Compartmentalized Information Facility, a SCIF, thousands of miles away.

"Hello," Logan answered.

"Stand by, let me go secure," Dodge stated and pressed SECDATA on the STE. They waited a few seconds until a secure line had been achieved. The display showed the session's classification level: LINE 1- Classified. "Can you hear us? You old Brass Rat?" David Dodge razzed his fellow MIT grad and former roommate.

"You old HAM, how are you?"

"I'm well. I've got your man, Cross, here with me. I'll let him respond to that. Tell him what you found," Dodge yielded the floor to Cross.

Cross cleared his throat. "Good morning...ah evening, Logan. I observed some interesting characteristics. Nothing conclusive, I'm afraid."

"Well, let's hear it," Logan said eagerly

"The fairing electronics are well sealed for exposure to water. That much we knew, but I did find that part of the electronics is a receiver."

"Like a radio? I thought it was a solar panel," Logan prompted.

Dodge spoke next. "It seems to be both. There is another way to convert light energy into electricity. Instead of viewing light as photons, light can be viewed as waves of electromagnetic radiation- just like radio waves only at a much higher frequency. The fairing seems to be made of countless tiny little antennae, each of which is roughly ¼ the wavelength of visible light allowing them to receive signals ranging from infrared all the way through ultra violet."

Cross continued. "Within the code, I was able to view a portion that indicated that the panel switches to a receiver function at sunset. At sunrise, the panels revert to generating energy with a traditional rectifying circuit."

"Ok. Did you learn anything more from the guidance and navigation perspective? Where was the fairing supposed to make landfall?" Logan inquired.

Cross wished he had more information for Logan. He hadn't got a chance to look more closely at that part of the code before he dozed off. The MSIC men had come too soon in the morning, and Cross hadn't had time to verify what he had observed. He wasn't confident he had given it a thorough look. All he had was a waypoint, perhaps. He expected to find a spot on land. He offered the information to Logan anyway.

"I found a coordinate in part of the guidance algorithm. Likely just a waypoint, because 9t seemed to indicate that the recovery location is in the Coral Sea, hundreds of miles from land."

"Yeah. That doesn't make sense. Perhaps the aero shells are picked up there by ship?" Logan posed a question.

"Maybe, but if you're making an ocean recovery, why not make it much closer to land? Save on fuel and transit time? There are a whole host of reasons. Even SpaceX returns its Dragon II Crew capsules to locations just off the shoreline so they can recover astronauts more easily. I'm afraid the coordinates may just be a waypoint or some interim navigation point. It's all we have to go on. MSIC officials arrived this AM to take the panels back to Huntsville."

Dodge wrapped up. "The boys from MSIC confirmed the launch was from Aurhihi Point in New Zealand. That can only be Rocket Sci."

And it if was Rocket Sci, and of Chinese origin, thought Cross, it was likely from a Solcom launch.

There was silence on the phone as Kraft mulled over the evidence.

"That's not very satisfying. I'm sorry we couldn't help solve your mystery, Archie." Cross felt like he had let Logan down.

"Cross," Logan addressed his employee. "How would you feel about traveling to Rocket Sci? We have a payload of our own due to launch with them sometime next year. I could arrange for you to visit to check in on that. It's a long shot. At least it would put you onsite. Our launch contract with Rocket Sci has provisions for supplier surveillance, but it's so far away, we rarely execute that clause."

"I'm at your disposal, sir."

"Ok, I'll have Christine set it up. Oh, and Cross, while I have you on a secure line, I'll need you back onsite next month for an out brief from the CIA on an investigation they started after your classified report on EV3. Something they're calling Project Palindrome." Kraft changed the topic again, "Archie, it was great to re-connect. Look me up if you ever come back East.

"You know, I will. Take care, Logan," said David.

"And Cross, good luck, but you won't need luck." Logan closed the secure line and was gone.

David depressed the speaker key to hang up the call. He removed the crypto card and placed it back into its carrying case. Cross was curious about the meeting Logan had just mentioned. Project Palindrome? Cross refocused his thoughts on the mysterious rocket solar panel.

The men exited the office building, boarded the Jeep-Kart, and drove to the airstrip. Cross reflected on all he had learned from Doctor Dodge. The mysterious island in the South Pacific that had gone silent key; the engaging history of the vanishing Sea Gull and her crew in 1836, which coincidently shared the HAM frequency of the island Dodge had yet to reach. Cross had learned about the importance of undersea fiber optic cables to the global internet infrastructure. He had been surprised and intrigued by the Ghost, Dodge's old supercavitation-driven "schooner." And, of course, there was the rocket fairing.

Cross had learned that it was part of a payload launched by the Chinese company Solcom. It was constructed of trillions of tiny little carbon nanotube antennas that made energy from sunlight in the day and listened for data at night.

What's more, he learned that the fairings floated and emitted light in the infrared spectrum. Cross was leaving Kwajalein with an enigmatic set of coordinates located somewhere in the middle of the Coral Sea. He couldn't help but feel like he was departing with more questions than he had when he arrived. He wished he had more time with the hardware before the MISC men had taken it away. Still, it was an enlightening visit, if nothing else. The new friends exchanged pleasantries plane side.

"Leaving so soon? You didn't even get a chance to take in all the sights."

All the sights? The atoll had an average height above sea level of 5 ft 11inches. The sea has reclaimed more and more land in recent years due to rising sea levels. If it weren't for the palm trees obstructing his view, Cross felt he could check that box by standing on his tiptoes to look around. He was eager for a venue change. Cross donned his small black and orange backpack as he bid farewell to Dodge.

"Thank you for the education, Doctor Dodge. I'll be sure to follow up with you if I learn more. I know how interested you are to have closure about the fairing."

"No, thank you. Good luck on your journey. Tell Logan, Best regards."

Cross boarded the small plane again. He had spent a lot of time in the air since leaving Dubai a few days ago. His next destination was Rocket Sci. He wondered if he would run into Alyne Jimmie, but he knew it was unlikely. The airshow was still in session. Undoubtedly, she would still be there in Dubai, and his time at Rocket

Sci would be brief. Cross wondered if the farewell message he had left with Rick Chan's silent subordinate had reached her.

| Chapter 9 |

Rocket Science

Ahuriri Point, Mahia Peninsula. New Zealand

Cross waited in the modern, well-decorated lobby for someone to greet him. Officially, his business at Rocket Sci was to discuss the progress of the launch his company had scheduled for next year. Logan had arranged his visit under the auspices of a supplier surveillance contract clause that allowed a representative to be onsite to oversee the final integration of their payload into Rocket Sci's delivery vehicle. Unofficially, Logan had asked him to gather any information he could about the Solcom solar panels installed on the inside of the rocket nose cone aeroshells. It was a favor to his boss's long-time college friend, and now it was Cross' mystery to solve.

The sample he had seen of New Zealand's north island on his way to Rocket Sci from the Auckland airport had impressed Cross. The landscape was pristine and beautiful. Pastures and farms lined the road with a backdrop of snow-capped mountains reminiscent of Austria and Switzerland a world away. Something about the New Zealand terrain made it distinct from those places. Cross couldn't quite place it. Perhaps, he thought, it was the contrast of rugged mountain terrain that flowed into farmland flats and finally to the ocean. There were few places in the world Cross could think of wherein a single glance, one could witness the transition of climate zones from treeless high altitude mountain peaks to seashores lined with palm trees. Or maybe, it was the sheep. Cross had heard that there were more sheep than people in New Zealand, and now he believed it. His rideshare driver had to slow or stop to let a wandering flock cross their path on more than one occasion. Here in this lobby, photos from all around the country lined the walls like a museum.

Cross stepped toward one photo for a closer look. A plaque below it read Fox Glacier, New Zealand, Te Waipounamu. The aerial shot showed a sweeping white glacier of ice cascading down through green mountains with pointed tops. Where the white sugar-coated ice stopped, a pure blue glacial ice melt met a river that ran between high cliff walls of a fjord, past palm trees, and into the sea. It was a landscape of surreal contrast. It was as if all the natural beauty icons of the world had been asked to huddle together for a photo and smile like they knew each other.

Another photo drew his attention. Columns of rock stacked in thin layers like pancakes rose out of the ocean along the coast. Waves broke against the bases of odd stone pillars, spraying a saltwater mist that cast a rainbow over the unique natural geological formation. The image's label read Punakaiki Rocks, Paparoa National Park. A man entered the conference room to greet him. Cross turned away from the gallery of foreign stills.

"Beck Peters, CEO of Rocket Sci, how do you do?" The man approached and introduced himself with a welcoming greeting. Beck's arm was outstretched in anticipation of a forthcoming handshake from ten paces away. "Ethan Cross, I presume?"

Cross stepped toward the man and arrested Beck's advance with a firm grasp of his hand. "Yes. Ethan Cross."

"You've come a long way, and on short notice, I might add. The message I received indicated you were in the vicinity. I must say, we don't get that a lot here on the Mahai Peninsula." The man offered a genuine and friendly laugh. "How can I help you?"

"Nearby may be a misnomer. I was on this side of the planet. A lot closer than any of my colleagues from the East Coast of the United States tend to venture often, so it was suggested I make a stop on my way home. Thank you for meeting me on short notice. My company has a launch with you early next year, and I was hoping to get some insight into the preparation activities."

Beck motioned for him to sit across from him at a set of high-end red leather armchairs positioned on either side of a modern coffee table. Between them on the coffee table stood a small sculpture, another piece of native Maori art. It was a stone carving of a green dragon emerging from water represented by fragments of shimmering multi-colored shells that caught the light. Its detail distracted Cross' attention.

"Well, I must say it's early for that. We typically marry payloads and nose assemblies to the booster stages between one month and a week before the launch date. Nonetheless, we are looking forward to launching your cargo. It'll be one of the first American defense projects that have gone up from here in some time." The CEO paused for a moment, realizing he might want to build the man's confidence in Rocket Sci's ability. "Rest assured, the predecessor entity, Rocket Lab, that operated here before Rocket Sci successfully launched countless defense-related satellites before moving to another site. We operate hardware of their design, and Launchpad One is a tried and true piece of infrastructure. Rocket Sci has busied itself as of late with scientific payloads sponsored by the Australian and New Zealand space agency as well as commercial launch contracts."

"Yes, I understand you have a contract to deliver a multi-satellite constellation to low earth orbit for a space-based internet service," Cross found an opportunity to mention his real reason for the visit, "Solcom's Icarus constellation?" Cross posed the question as he eyed the small sculpture between them.

"Ah, yes. Solcom has been a primary customer in recent years." Cross felt the CEO sizing up Cross' intentions. Cross was keenly aware that the businessman would naturally try to understand if his visit was the precursor to a new business opportunity or just a glad-hand moment to maintain an existing relationship with an established customer. He didn't want to mislead the man. Dishonesty made him sick. He knew how it felt to be on the receiving end of deception. It wouldn't be necessary; the CEO seemed to sense Cross was not a new business prospect as he continued, "Our launch today is one of theirs, in fact. And we are in the middle of marrying their next nose cone payload assembly to a rocket for another upcoming launch." Mr. Peters noticed Cross was distracted by the intricate decoration between them. He decided to offer some trivia.

"It's a Maori jade carving." Beck indulged his guest with a detour. "The Maori people who were first to occupy this land tell of the legendary Taniwha Dragon, which appears in their ancient legends and is often depicted in their carvings. In Maori cultures, carvings carry a story. Native Maori didn't have a written language. Each carving tells a tale. Dragons are benevolent protectors that watch over us and control the world's oceans. These Hei Matau carvings symbolize a safe journey over water. "

"And this turquoise material?" Cross pointed to the watery fragments of tile.

"The water is made from Paua shell. Paua is harvested from the Coral Sea's pristine clear coastal waters of New Zealand. The waters are rich in minerals, which give the Paua shell its intense depth of color. It's quite rare because Paua is protected by a quota system and by controlling the equipment used by the quota holders who must "free dive" for their quotas."

"Free dive?" asked Cross.

"Yes. Freediving is diving without the use of air tanks. Although now I understand it's permissible to use a small class of compressed air tanks that can be held to your mouth, which affords a few more minutes of dive time. It's challenging to collect Paua, nonetheless."

Cross imagined what it must be like to dive in the shallow pure ocean water, searching for such a beautiful treasure.

"It's a magnificent piece. What is this curled-up fern shape?"

"The Koru. It depicts a fern frond's unfolding and represents a celebration of the vitality of life, of new replacing old. Fresh beginnings." The CEO checked his comm-band and continued. "Speaking of fresh beginnings, there is a rocket launch that demands my attention. What more can I help you with, Mr. Cross?"

Cross replied. "Do you offer a tour of your facility?"

"Yes. I might suggest viewing a typical payload to booster assembly while you are here."

Cross nodded, "Perfect. That's just what I had in mind."

"Good as gold then. Our rockets are assembled indoors, laying down on their side. You can view much from the protective glass of our customer lounge. I think it'll be representative of the process your hardware will experience when the time comes." The busy CEO stood. "I'm afraid I'll have to hand you off to one of our mission integration and launch coordination specialists. I'll arrange for one to greet you here." Cross stood as well. "It was very nice to meet you, Mr. Cross. Rocket Sci is looking forward to working with you and your company more in the future. Please help yourself to some tea. It'll be just a few minutes."

"Thank you again for the education," Cross motioned to the jade dragon surrounded by paua shell.

"Choice. Think nothing of it. May the Taniwha grant you a safe journey home over the sea. Goodbye, or as we say here Kia ora." The CEO turned and left the lobby. Cross nodded politely in acknowledgment as Beck sped away.

Cross wandered back to the collection of photographs returning his attention to the picture gallery on the lobby wall. The neighboring photo was equally stunning. It was a starscape of the night sky with blue light points that had a depth like Cross had never seen. The center of the image showed such exquisite detail; he felt he could dive into the cosmos before him. Cross was aware that the night sky from the southern hemisphere would be unfamiliar, but the image looked alien. He could feel the depth of the universe pulling him in. Nearer constellations seemed closer and more focused, while layers of distance blue twinkling stars receded.

"It's not a photo of the stars if that's what you're wondering." The voice behind Cross was a woman's. Cross turned. He recognized her in an instant.

"Miss Alyne Jimmie." Cross greeted his ski companion from Dubai a few days earlier with enthusiasm, "I'm surprised to see you back here so soon."

"Ethan Cross. Small world. Whatever brings you here?" Alyne shook his hand firmly, finishing her comment. "That's a photo of the inside of the glow-worm cave system at Waitomo here on the North Island. Lots of visitors ask if it's a picture of the stars."

"Glow worms? I've never heard of such a thing." Cross mentioned.

"Ah, yes. It's a natural wonder. The worms live on the ceiling of caves. Their glow is biolume or bioluminescence. The insect species is more closely related to spiders than worms, actually. They use the light to attract their prey, which gets caught in a silky lure like a spider's web. Nothing like that in Australia, but I've had a chance to see them for myself since coming to work for Rocket Sci. I spend a great deal of time here in New Zealand overseeing launches."

"I imagine. I caught the beginning of your speech at the airshow before I had to depart. Impressive. You must have left to return shortly after that as well?" Cross inquired.

"Oh, yes. I finished my address and left the following

morning on a supersonic into Nancy Bird with a conventional connection back to Auckland. I had to be back for the Solcom launch today. It's the last for another few weeks. No time for me to linger at the airshow, I'm afraid. I'll have a bit of a break after this launch, though. And you? What brings you here?"

Cross decided to ditch his cover story. Alyne was undoubtedly in a position to shed some light on the rocket fairing mystery.

"My boss sent me here to inquire about a rocket aero shell that was recovered in the sea. It appears to be part of the nose cone of a Solcom rocket launched from here."

"Well, that can't be right; Solcom's fairings would burn up on reentry, like any other. Fairings are expendable; each launch consumes them. It's too expensive for us to design a recovery system as larger Rockets use."

"I can assure you; I've seen one. It's most definitely not expendable. It's got a solar panel built into it; a unique solar panel."

"Then it's not Solcom's. Follow me, and I'll show you. We have another one of their payloads in final integration now. It's due to launch a few weeks after today's." Alyne said confidently and led her guest through a door at the rear of the lobby into a long corridor. He noted her resistance to his assertion. Cross wondered if she'd ever seen a Solcom payload outside its final enclosure.

"Have you ever seen the interior of the fairings themselves?"

"No, the nose cones are installed by Solcom enclosing the payload before it arrives here at Rocket Sci, but I do know that Solcom's design was achieved with great collaboration with Rocket Sci engineers. The fineness ratio, or the length of a nose cone compared to its base, was a significant challenge with their spiral design. Our designers provided a lot of insight a few years ago to ensure they achieved an outer mold line of the proper caliber for the nose cone. Of course, they are the first customer we've allowed to design their payload enclosure to our external specifications. They have a unique spiral separation line that follows the contour, but it's still a Haack."

"A Hack?"Cross questioned. Surely she didn't mean it was designed quickly at the expense of quality or attention to detail. Somewhere in that statement, there was an ironic joke to be made. There was some humor to be had contrasting the precision of rocket science with the job being a hack.

"Yeah, it is a traditional Haack series design that minimizes aerodynamic drag," Alyne carried on as he followed. Cross was glad he hadn't made a pun out of that. She knew what she was talking about. She ushered him into a meeting space with a grand glass barrier separating them from a clean-room area beyond where engineers in white hooded suits were inspecting the rocket top assembly. The fuselage lay prone on its side. "Have a look, no solar panels," Alyne said, stretching her arm out to present the view.

Cross saw men and women viewing the specimen. They looked like astronauts orbiting around the space vehicle in the setting. The helmeted suits were required to maintain class 100,000 clean room protocols, where the concentration of contaminant particles was tightly controlled. From the viewing area of the segregated client suite, Alyne and Cross gazed at the spacecraft.

"Alyne. I've seen the inside surface of the fairings. Solcom has installed a solar panel on the inside." Cross provided the surprising detail.

"Really!? The inside? That doesn't make sense. Why invest that kind of design work into something that'll be discarded?"

"They aren't discarded." He stood near the glass window and pointed at the separation lines. "The inside of each seam has a control surface aileron tucked in behind the adjacent one. I'm not confident about the coordinates, but I think they are guided to a recovery spot in the Coral Sea."

"That's intriguing. We've been launching these for a few years. I had no idea. Solcom must be retrieving their hardware after launch." Alyne looked from Cross through the viewing window of the customer lounge. She thought for a moment, "I may be able to cross-reference who is supplying Solcom with solar panels in the registry of suppliers that Solcom is required to submit to us. I wonder what they are being used for? I'll have time after the countdown. Would you like to watch the launch?"

"Would I ever!" Cross excitement was a mixture of professional enthusiasm and schoolboy glee. He had never seen a rocket launch from up close.

T-Minus 5 minutes.

Across Hawkes bay from Mahia Peninsula, Albert and Sean dialed in their telescopes and aimed them at the familiar Ahuriri Point launch pad. The amateur rocket watchers were excited for the launch a few minutes away. They focused their attention intently across Hawke's bay, noting a bright alternating green and red flashing light they hadn't seen before emanating from the control tower.

The father and son rocketeers discussed the new statistics they would record on the behavior of the fairings they had recently observed. They wanted more evidence of the supposed recovery to post on their club forum. They were installing a digital video camera they had just purchased into Sean's Cassegrain telescope when something unusual drew their attention to the water over Hawke's Bay.

A white, high winged business jet with a slight jog in the curve of its belly entered their field of view. It crossed the bay from East to West in a descending glide slope toward Napier.

The Clifton rocketeers didn't need their instruments to observe the scene unfolding in front of them.

"Papa, I think it's going to crash in the harbor!"

"No, son, it's a flying boat. It's going to land on the bay."

"I've never seen an airplane land on the water."

The amphibious aircraft terminated its shallow 3-degree glide slope with a kiss on the calm ocean bay. It skipped twice before settling into a wake that slowed it to the pace of a speed boat. It motored on toward the coastal city. Albert spoke to his son.

"Planes have been landing on the water for hundreds of years, son. Before airports were built, flying boats filled the sky. I wouldn't be surprised if our own aviatrix, Nancy Bird herself, even piloted one into remote locations in the bush over two hundred years ago back in the 1930s."

"Who is Nancy Bird?" The young boy asked his father.

"Nancy Bird? The angel of the outback? Why she's Australia's very own Amelia Earhart."

"Who is Amelia Earhart?" Sean asked his father with innocent eyes.

T-minus 2 minutes.

From a few miles away, safely behind the glass of Rocket Sci's launch observation deck, Cross stared at the black obelisk covered with white frost poised for liftoff at the end of Ahuriri Point. The separation lines wrapping around the tip reminded him of a soft-serve ice cream. Cross knew the ice on the exterior of the two-stage launch vehicle resulted from the condensation of the humid coastal air on the fuselage, cooled by the fuel within. The spacecraft had been topped off with liquid oxygen and rocket-grade kerosene and was ready to drill through the thin atmosphere above.

"Marvelous, isn't it, that just a few minutes after launch, and the second stage will deliver its contents of internet communications satellites to low earth orbit?" Alyne offered over his shoulder. "It looks like an iced coffee, doesn't it?"

Cross thought it was an odd reference. "I thought it looks more like the top of a soft-serve ice cream."

"Naw, Yeah. Ice cream with a side of cake! We're about to light the candle. Nine of them." Alyne said with excitement in her voice. "There are nine Rutherford engines on the first stage. One more will carry the second stage and its contents to orbit. It'll be too high by then to see the fairings separate with the naked eye. We might be able to review the radar telemetry after launch. However, we are primarily set up to gather telemetry on the first and second-stage trajectories since the fairings are of no value to track. I'll collect you a few minutes after lift-off. Enjoy the show." Alyne hurried off to join the team, manning the final countdown. Cross turned back to the window.

T-minus 1 minute.

Cross watched as small streams of gas vented from the lower first stage. In the background, he heard a status announcement over the machinery of his mind.

"Stage 1 tanks pressed."

He saw another two puffs of gas condense as they exhausted the final ounces of fuel, ensuring the propellant was filled to the max.

"Stage 2 tanks are pressed."

T-minus 30 seconds.

Cross heard another announcement as he noticed a thick cable attached midway up the fuselage.

"High flow engine purge enabled."

The support tower structure was retracted 5 minutes earlier, leaving only a cable of hoses and wires tethering the vehicle to the planet. More words filled the silence of anticipation.

"Deluge activated."

Cross looked on as gallons of water began to pour under the nine rocket motors, ready to ignite in seconds. He knew the water was to protect the fuselage from the percussive vibration damage, muffling the sound of the roaring Rutherford engines. He wondered if the acoustic suppression measures offered any other noise abatement benefits on this remote peninsula. Besides the sheep, thought Cross, the nearest people would be miles from the pad.

"Five, four, three, two, one. Ignition."

Plumes of water vaporized into steam as the powerful engines thrust the tapered cylinder off the surface of the launch pad. The cable, the rocket's last link to its terrestrial origin, released and fell away against the launch tower. The engines worked in powerful unison, looking like one single jet of bright, superheated fire laughing at the earth as it ascended faster and faster. It cleared the cloud of steam and rose to the heavens. The rocket was halfway up the glass in front of Cross when the signature rumble engulfed him. The sound of launch saturated his ears and reverberated in his chest. He wasn't watching a rocket launch; he was feeling it. The craft disappeared through a high layer of cirrostratus clouds propelled by chemistry and accomplishment.

Alyne broke his concentration as he craned his neck to follow the spacecraft to the top of the window sill of the observation deck grand viewport.

"It'll be traveling almost 9000 Kilometer per hour in another couple of minutes when the fairings separate at nearly 120 kilometers above us." Alyne offered, peering up over his shoulder. "No chance of seeing them, especially with that cloud cover."

"That was incredible. New replaces used, young replaces old, the evidence is as natural as seasons change. Progress is made." Cross quoted the final words he remembered of Alyne's speech days earlier, casting a smirk in her direction.

"You paid attention to my speech, did you?" Alyne

said with professional modesty as a blush rose to her cheeks.

"Don't you have a launch to attend to?" Cross teased the mission director.

"It was a routine launch save for a small plane approaching Napier we had to light signal to keep away. It's pretty much fire and forget after lift-off, Mr. Cross," Alyne informed him. "This launch vehicle system has been in continuous operation since the first Electron Rocket launches in the second decade of 2000. A US company called Rocket Lab licensed the delivery system design to Rocket Sci. It sold this facility to us as a commercial extension subsidized by the New Zealand and Australian Space agencies, over a decade ago when Rocket Lab moved onto a new launch site and more modern equipment."

"Are you saying that rocket we just witnessed is a 30-year-old design?" Cross was impressed.

"Yes, but it's reliable. If it ain't broke, don't fix it. And besides, we aren't working with NASA budgets here, Mr. Cross. We need launches to be cheap and routine to keep the lights on around here."

She motioned for him to follow her back to the client suite. Alyne called up the registry of suppliers submitted by Solcom on the glass board. She and Cross scanned the list together. It was expansive—hundreds of suppliers were listed in alphabetical order. The scrolling list mesmerized the detectives. After a few minutes, they reached the N's.

"I should tell you something else about the fairings." Cross thought it might help them screen the list of vendors. "The panel switches modes at night. It becomes a receiver of some sort in the dark."

"That certainly adds to the mystery, doesn't it?" Alyne looked perplexed. "This is feeling more and more like a detective thriller, isn't it, Sherlock?"

"Sherlock?" Cross smiled inquisitively at Alyne.

"Yeah, it's your case, so you're Sherlock Holmes." Alyne teased.

"I guess that makes you Watson then," Cross played along with a smile while his eyes remained trained on the scrolling list of supplier names on the glass board in front of them.

"Wait. Stop." Said Cross. "There. NoviX."

"NoviX? Isn't that the same supplier that provides panels to the Intellagama?" Cross made the connection to the aircraft that was headlining the Dubai airshow earlier that week.

"Yes. I recall Rick Chan mentioning that." Alyne searched NoviX on the glass board. The glass board displayed a hit that confirmed Cross' memory. NoviX is a vendor of nanomanufacturing solar technology.

Alyne spoke up, "I wonder if NoviX panel technology is exportable? Nanomanufacturing technology may not be something Australian companies can sell outside the commonwealth. We need to make certain that Rocket Sci complies with Australia's equivalent to your International Traffic in Arms Regulations (ITAR) and the Export Administration Regulations (EAR)."

"Ok," replied Cross. "How do We do that?" We? He thought. Cross was cautious about taking on a partner after his experience in London.

"I don't have to oversee another launch for three

weeks. I plan to head back to Sydney. I can get more information on NoviX and their supplier status with Rocket Sci from our supplier management records at Rocket Sci's headquarters. How'd you like to accompany me to Sydney?"

Cross preferred to work alone. His thoughts swirled with hesitation. The last time he partnered up didn't turn out well. He had no reason not to trust her. Still, he considered the offer. Maybe teaming up with Alyne would allow him to provide more clues to Logan and Dr. Dodge. More time with Alyne didn't sound altogether unpleasant. Cross decided to take the case.

"Sounds like a mystery with intrigue, Doctor Watson." He echoed her playful charade, suspending his hesitation to team up in favor of the opportunity to gain access to more data. "The game is afoot." He smiled back at his fellow detective.

| Chapter 10 |

Another Emerald City

Sydney. Australia

Alyne hailed a rideshare from her comm-specs as their plane taxied to park at the jetway. In no time, they were stepping to the curbside pick-up zone of the modern Nancy-Bird Walton Airport. Despite being in service for nearly two decades since it was built in 2026, Sydney's "new" airport still looked the part. It was a gateway to their continent. Or as the playwright, David Williamson famously wrote of Sydney in 1987, "Welcome to the Emerald City of Oz. Everyone comes here along their yellow brick roads looking for the answers to their problems, and all they find are the demons within themselves."

Cross marveled at the modern airport terminal. It was built on the city's outskirts, where the available real estate afforded the futuristic structure to stretch out in all directions. Its long runways had been upgraded to support supersonic airliners from all over the world.

Australians were as proud of the facility as they were of Nancy-Bird Walton herself. Cross learned from a plaque on a statue of the woman in the center of the expansive Airport promenade that in 1933, at age 18,

Nancy-Bird had become the youngest woman in the Commonwealth to hold a commercial pilot's license. She was Australia's most pioneering aviator. Nancy-Bird was an inspiration and not just to women, to everyone. She had bought her own plane and began transporting the sick from isolated regions around the country, landing on whatever grass patch was available helping to set up the Royal Flying Doctors' Service. Before her death in 2009, she was awarded the Order of Australia. Imagine, Cross thought, how much more of an impact she could have with today's technology like the Intellagama, which could land and take off in even more remote places without needing a sprawling airport infrastructure like the one they were now exiting. Cross watched Rocket Sci's Director of Launch and Mission Integration heave her large framed backpack onto the roof of the vintage Range Rover. He smiled as he thought Nancy would be proud. Maybe one day, Australia would look back on Alyne as another pioneering woman.

"Did you pack anything in that tiny bag?" Alyne pointed at Cross' small backpack, "under-roos, I hope?"

"I find there are few things I can travel with that outweigh the benefit of traveling lite. Just my comm-pad, some business attire, and, of course, my superman under-roos." She and Cross shared a laugh as they climbed aboard the well-equipped automobile. He kept his small bag with him.

Cross admired the off-road vehicle as he navigated around it to where the driver's seat should have been.

The safari-ready rig had a rugged steel roof cage and a snorkel for an old internal combustion engine's air intake. The 4x4 vehicle had a prominent front bumper with a crash bar full of lights. The grill guard reminded Cross of the cowcatcher on the front of an old steam locomotive. He would ask the driver about that. Their ride exuded the character of Australia. Cross admired that Sydney still allowed internal combustion-powered cars. It was one of the only modern cities that hadn't yet banned them in favor of electric vehicles.

"G'Day, mates. It says you're heading to the business district by Hyde Park?" The driver confirmed Rocket Sci headquarters' address that Alyne had transmitted from the plane as they settled into their seats. Cross sat shotgun on the truck's left side where the steering wheel should have been.

"That's right," Alyne confirmed, from behind the driver to Cross' right.

"What's with the massive Safari bumper on your truck?" Cross asked their new chauffeur.

"It's for the roos!" He responded enthusiastically as he steered the vehicle toward downtown.

"What? There can't be that many kangaroos in Sydney." Cross said, figuring the accessory was more for looks than for function.

"Naw, Yeah, Mate. It's not for Sydney; it's for the

Outback."

"Seriously? How often do you drive through the wilderness?"

"I drive out to Uluru-Kata Tjuta at least once a month. It's a big tourist attraction, and," the driver paused as he concentrated on navigating traffic without autopilot, "It's not the wilderness. Here, we call it the Bush. My girlfriend works there as a park ranger. We don't have Safaris in Straya. She leads Outback Expeditions."

"Uluru-Kata, What is that?" Cross asked.

"Ayers Rock. It's a 2200 km drive to the heart of Australia." The driver patted his steering wheel. "She's saved me from the roos a number o' times."

Cross figured that was about 1400 miles. Roughly half the distance across the United States. To drive there must take at least a day and a half, maybe two. "How long does that take to make that drive?"

"Four or five days. It's a grueling trip." The driver provided a duration longer than Cross expected.

"Five days? That's longer than it takes to drive from New York to LA, which is twice as far." Cross offered data that shed some doubt on the driver's claim. He wondered if the roads were poorly maintained in the Outback?

"Right on, Mate. But we don't drive at night."

Cross looked at all the extra headlights mounted all over the Outback Expedition vehicle. "Oh yeah? Why's that?"

"The roos 'll take you out." The driver said matter-of-factly.

Alyne offered confirmation, "Yes, they're all over at night, they're like your squirrels, only they can weigh as much as 100 kilos and stand 3 meters tall."

"Wow, that does sound like a dangerous trip. And what about the snorkel?" Cross pointed at the ductwork affixed to the passenger side windscreen, outside along the A-pillar.

"The reason for the breather is we can get a lot of rain up here in a short amount of time. Better to be prepared when you're in the Bush."

"Things are pretty extreme here in Australia," Cross responded, looking back at Alyne.

Alyne offered a knowing smile.

Cross took in foreign sights for nearly an hour as the setting evolved from suburbs to urban. The driver piloted the safari vehicle through a northern approach route into Australia's largest city. Their captain navigated the M4 to the M7 to the M2, where the 4x4 passed a sign for

Manly Beach. The driver noticed Cross reading the sign and offered some trivia to the man from out of town.

"Some call her the Emerald City, but I prefer Harbor City. Sydney is a city of beaches. There are more than 100 beaches for Sydneysiders."

"That's impressive," Cross replied, keeping an eye out for a view of the Harbor Bridge.

"If we have time after our meeting, I'll take you to one," Alyne added from the back.

"Ok. I'd love to see the Opera house too if there's a chance. I think that's a required stop for a tourist."

The driver directed Cross' attention to the view ahead. "Looks like you can check that box sooner than you think, Mate."

As the driver merged onto the M1, the occupants got their first glimpse of the famous steel arch of the Sydney Harbor Bridge. The Opera House's white scallops appeared just beyond and below the bridge. The iconic structure was synonymous with the city. Cross had read that the designer was inspired by nature, the shape of shells and a peeled orange. It reminded Cross more of his recent time in Dubai, another Emerald City, and the sailboat-inspired architecture of the Al Arab Hotel and its dhow sail silhouette.

Cross refocused his attention on the Harbor Bridge in

the foreground. He noticed something he didn't expect atop the structure's towering arches.

"Are those people standing on top of the bridge?" Cross blurted out with surprise.

"Yeah, Mate! It's a tour. Perhaps you should make that another stop on your punch card?"

"A tour? Scaling a bridge? This place is extreme." Cross' view lingered on the tiny row of people filing like ants high above. Soon he was distracted by a phenomenal view of the Opera House to his left.

Their outback expedition vehicle had crossed the bridge, passed by the tranquil Darling Harbor, and arrived at the north entrance to Hyde Park. Alyne addressed the driver.

"Let us out here. Our building is straight through the Park on the south side. We have time for a short walk."

The driver obliged and beat Alyne and Cross to her pack, pulling it down from the roof rack and presenting it to her cordially. "Have a great stay, Mates. Watch out for them roos."

Hyde Park was seasoned and distinctive. An old-growth of exotic-looking fig trees lined the main promenade and ran the park's quarter-mile length. The trees' branches stretched to reach each other across a wide central walkway forming a natural corridor.

Parisian-style lamp posts with white balls accentuated the path on either side of the tunnel of greenery.

As the pair of gumshoes began their trek through the historic promenade, a black electric taxi silently accelerated away. It had released its occupant just beyond where the outback expedition vehicle had departed moments before. The occupant started a brisk walk toward the park's central fountain. He matched pace with Cross and Alyne but stayed far behind. The shade of the fig branches kept the intense Australian sun from searing his hairless head.

After a few minutes, the pair approached the park's central feature, the Archibald Fountain. A hexagon-shaped pool encircled a muscular nude statue. The stone figure stood on a pillar in a classic Greco pose at the pool's center. The fountain cast dramatic streams of water like rays of the sun in a fan shape, framing the poised man like the tail of a peacock. Alyne pointed at the statue and offered some trivia as they passed.

"It's Apollo. The semi-circle of water jets behind him are rays of light spread out to depict the rising sun. I read the inscription once on a lunch break. It refers to the sun as the Star of Day." The pair continued past the fountain as Cross responded.

"Seems like an appropriate reference for us on our way to inquire about solar panels used on a spacecraft."

"I thought you might think so," Alyne stated, leading

them down the central path extending the length of the park beyond Apollo. Cross stole a glance to his left at a massive gothic cathedral that reminded Cross of Notre Dame in Paris. He looked right and up through the trees catching a glimpse of Sydney's Tower Eye. It stood over one thousand feet above them. It was taller than the Seattle Space Needle and far taller than Rocket Sci's old Electron Rocket, but looking up at the tower reminded him of the launch he had witnessed earlier nonetheless.

The trees beyond the fountain formed another wide natural tunnel. Soon they approached a low reflection pool. The ornamental water feature ran the length of the walkway. The strip of still water reflected the sky and the trees on either side like a mirror. Cross could see large dark-colored fig fruits hanging from the trees' branches above in the reflection of the calm water. He looked up to the trees and directly at the fruit. He had never seen a fig before. The figs were as big as footballs or larger and speckled the branches as far down the leafy tunnel as he could see. Beyond the canopy of branches, Cross could see a few more adorning the trees that lined the reflection pool where the sky spilled in over the water ahead.

Behind them, far to their left, beyond where a casual glance to the side might see him, a bald Polynesian man tracked the partners from behind comm-specs. The Polynesian followed the pair, choosing a path across the shallow water from the man and woman bound for Rocket Sci.

Cross and Alyne were midway the pool's length when Alyne motioned ahead to the skyline at the park's end. She pointed at one of the taller modern buildings, just off-center from the walk. It stood slightly shorter than the Sydney Tower.

"That's it. There is Rocket Sci headquarters."

"Impressive." Cross followed the structure from the ground to its peak with his eyes. "That's your building?" Cross asked.

"Naw, Yeah, we can't afford a building like that. We don't have deep-pocket customers like Space Force in these parts. We rent the top floors, but it's no schelp."

Just as Alyne finished her comment, Cross sensed motion in his peripheral vision through the open side of his comm-specs. Peripheral vision is more sensitive to movement and changes in brightness. A bald pedestrian on the opposite side of the pool had stepped on a fallen twig. The snap of the branch could be heard crisply across the water. He turned his head to see a large dark fig fruit falling from a tree limb on the opposite side of the reflection pool. At first, its reflection moved away from Cross at the same rate as the fruit fell, but suddenly the reflection stopped moving. He looked directly at the falling fruit. It sprouted wings two feet long on either side and headed straight toward him and Alyne. It swooped low over the reflection pool, kissed the water, flapped, and turned away just ahead of the pedestrians revealing a jagged webbed profile stretched between arms with clawed hands. The creature had a triangular head with a pointed snout. Beady black eyes stared darkly at Cross as it ascended to a spot on another tree branch where it settled and took its place hanging near other large fig fruit. Cross stopped in his tracks.

"What. Was. That!?"

"A flying Fox. You've never seen a bat, Mr. Cross?" Alyne asked, laughing at Cross' misplaced alarm.

"A flying fox!? We have bats the size of mice! Not vampire bats with a four-foot wingspan! Look," Cross pointed to a handful of other branches, "they're all over the trees. I thought those were figs!"

"Figs are the size of mice, Ethan. All of those are fox bats." Alyne was full-on laughing now, "You should have seen your face."

Cross laughed back, "I may need to change my under roos." Cross joked.

"Hope you have a Batman pair, you Bogan." Alyne laughed and led the foreigner ahead to Rocket Sci.

"Extreme Australia." He said, shaking off the startle.

The shadowy pursuer watched the detectives approach the lobby of the tall structure. Outwardly, he made no expression of his relief that his miss-step on a fallen branch hadn't drawn the attention of his prey.

Thankfully, the fox bat had taken their attention away from the man. He kept his focus on the inside surface glass of his comm-specs, reached for a familiar button on the ear stay, snapped a photo, and transmitted the image

At the top floor of Rocket Sci's headquarters, they were greeted by a receptionist. Alyne left her pack at the desk; Cross opted to wear his. They were shown to a conference room where they waited for Rocket Sci's export control officer and the supply chain lead. The pair had a grand view of the Opera House beyond the green expanse of Hyde Park that they had just traversed from within a small room. Cross and Alyne were a few minutes early for the meeting. Their hosts arrived on time, prepared with answers to the questions Alyne had sent in advance. Christian Malack, Rocket Sci's supplier management director, entered the room speaking.

"Good Day, Miss Jimmie. We pulled our records on NoviX. It turns out that the only other artifact we've received from Solcom besides their registry of suppliers is a statement that NoviX supplies solar panels. Solar panels have no export restrictions, so we never flagged the item as an ITAR concern." Rocket Sci's supply chain lead started.

"That's what I was afraid of." Alyne responded, "This is Ethan Cross. He's with an American defense contractor with which we do business. He's been asked to look into Solcom and NoviX as well."

"Good to meet you, Mr. Cross." Christian shook his

hand. "Christian Malack. Supply Chain." They all sat as the second man offered some information.

"NoviX's unique nanomanufacturing technology is export controlled. Export law prohibits them from selling the core technology to countries outside the commonwealth or sharing the technical know-how to manufacture. Cameron Syme, Export Compliance." He offered his hand to Ethan and then to Alyne, who he knew well.

"Ethan Cross." Cross acknowledged the man's greeting. "NoviX panels are built into the Intellagama Electric jet. An Australian company called MagiX builds them and delivers them in conjunction with the Chinese, who supply the engines and sell the aircraft worldwide. How does NoviX work that deal?"

"Yes. I looked into that. MagiX can sell products containing NoviX technology, but not to just anyone. The Australian Government closely monitors its international sales. MagiX has a special agreement allowing them to sell the jet commercially, but there are provisos that prohibit NoviX from selling replacement panels directly to end customers." Syme turned to address Alyne.

"Rocket Sci may be exposed if NoviX hasn't sought the same permissions or filed for an Australian General Export License, an AUSGEL." Cameron looked at Cross. "It's similar to the US State Department's Technical Assistance Agreement. It would allow NoviX to supply to a Chinese firm like Solcom. Rocket Sci would normally request this type of paperwork from suppliers for any product flagged as export-controlled to ensure all suppliers comply with Export laws. Still, as you heard from Mr. Malack, we thought they were just a merchant supplier of vanilla, solar panels." Cameron subtlety indicated that the blame for the oversight was on the supply chain organization, not on his export compliance team.

Alyne spoke next. "Have you inquired with the Australian Department of Defense Export Administration about NoviX's standing?" Alyne knew the Australian DoD administered export law.

"Not yet. The agency is notoriously slow to respond, and besides, we'd prefer to have our own house in order first. It would be best for us to inquire through Solcom or directly with NoviX before involving the authorities. We should get all our ducks in a row, you know." Syme suggested as he looked at Malack.

"I've received no response from Solcom on the matter. I've already sent a message to Mr. Roger Morrison, my counterpart in NoviX supplier management, to inquire about their export permissions-No response yet." Malack stated to show he was on the ball.

"Is there anything else?" Alyne asked the gentlemen.

"We don't have any other records on file here. I'm sorry we couldn't be of more help," stated Syme.

"Do you think NoviX or Solcom is deliberately hiding something?" asked Cross.

Syme asked a question as he formulated a response, "What business is Solcom in again?"

"Solcom is a satellite-based internet service provider," said Cross, "they transfer high volumes of data between LEO satellites using lasercomm and transmit it to the ground."

Malack spoke next. He asked. "LEO?"

Cross answered politely. "Low Earth Orbit. Satellites whizzing by as low as 250 miles overhead like Solcom's can only download data to a ground station once every hour or two. Some LEO satellites are only able to release data they've gathered once each day."

"Why is that?" Malack pressed.

"Each one circles the planet every 90 minutes or completes a full orbit once every two hours. They can only see a small segment of the earth's surface beneath them at their low altitude. Because of the speed they travel across the sky, a pass over any point on the ground only lasts 8 or 9 minutes."

"They transfer data between satellites using lasers, you say?" Syme interjected. "That could eliminate costly regulatory and spectrum licensing hurdles. Obtaining a radio frequency license for global usage these days is nearly impossible and at the very least expensive, prohibitively expensive as I understand."

Syme rubbed his chin. "One thing I've observed in the export compliance business over the years is that if there is a technology that her Majesty can realize an economic benefit from exporting, she will find a way. I'm not suggesting she is turning a blind eye or neglecting her duties, but she has limited resources and must choose her priorities. Clearly, the Commonwealth has invested much effort to properly arrange NoviX's nano-technology export through MagiX for the Intellagama. Perhaps they believe they can say they've done their due diligence? After all, the outback still has poor internet coverage. It wouldn't hurt Oz for our own native technology to improve that situation, even if it required foreign help. Maybe Solcom is delivering the NoviX solar panels to someone using our rockets?"

"It is a capital mistake to theorize before one has data, wouldn't you agree, Mr. Holmes?" Alyne winked at Cross. Cross winked back. She was right. Syme's conjecture was a heavy dose of government conspiracy theory.

Nonetheless, Cross had seen a far more egregious example of government graft with the UK Ministry of Defense concerning EV3, their CEO Cain, and the ARCELOR. Alyne's comment made him keep his thought to himself, *could Solcom be delivering the NoviX panels to themselves to avoid exports laws? But what for? Launching them to the edge of space on a rocket seemed like an elaborate means to avoid customs regulations.*

Alyne was right. They needed more data.

"If that's all we have, I guess a visit to NoviX is in order." Alyne stated bluntly, "we follow the trail of clues to its logical conclusion. Let me see if there are any flights to Brisbane. I'll be back momentarily" She stood and turned back to Malack and Syme, undeterred by the dead end. "Thank you, Gentlemen. I'll let you know what we find at NoviX." She stood and exited the room. The two men sat up, exchanged pleasantries with Cross, and left the room behind her.

So they may be following the scent to Brisbane next, thought Cross. He stood in the vacant room as he waited for Alyne to return. He couldn't deny Alyne's Sherlock Holmes parallel. Whatever Solcom was doing with the NoviX panels was still a mystery to him. Cross stared out the window across the flying fox sanctuary of Hyde Park and at the famous scalloped landmark beyond. Cross remembered he had a good friend who lived in Brisbane. Maybe they could look him up.

"Well," said Alyne as she reentered the room, "it looks like the soonest we can leave would be a morning flight. It's Friday. We can't get there before they close, so we'll have to shoot for when they open on Monday. The same flight runs on Sunday, too, so we either stay here in Sydney for a couple of nights, or we find a place in Brisbane for Saturday and Sunday."

"I have a college buddy that lives in Brisbane," Cross thought a Saturday night with his old friend sounded fun,

"I could look him up."

"That may work," agreed Alyne.

"If we go out in the morning, what time will we arrive in Brisbane?" Cross asked.

"Just before lunchtime on Saturday."

"Ok, I'll get in touch with him. What'll we do until the flight tomorrow?" Cross hoped they could check out the renowned Sydney Opera at the edge of the famous harbor.

"We show you Sydney. That's what we do." Alyne responded with a smile. "I know just the place."

"The Opera House?" Cross made the obvious guess.

"Naw, Yeah. You'll get your fix of the Opera House, but I mean Bondi. We're getting you Pie Face, and I'm taking you to Bondi." Alyne said with enthusiasm.

"Bondi? What's that?"

"Between the Flags? You don't know? Well," Alyne smiled, "I'll show you. Let's get some grub, see the Opera House, hit Coogee, and do Bondi."

"Ok," Cross agreed, not quite sure what he had signed up for. "What is Pie Face?"

"You'll see." Alyne led the way out. Cross followed questions swirling in his head. Between the Flags? Hit Coogee? Do Bondi?

Alyne had a secretary book their flights for the following morning, and the pair of detectives headed out for a Sydney city tour. Soon they exited the fox bat invested fig tree gauntlet toward Harbor Bridge when Alyne made a victorious declaration.

"There! Pie Face." She pointed ahead at a small, fast food storefront.

"Oh, you mean Pie. Dessert for Lunch?" Ethan saw a smiley face logo printed on a large plastic pie, followed by the text *Pie Face* on the corner store. Another smiley face was visible within the letter A within the word Face. Clever, thought Cross.

"Not Lollies. Meat. Pie Face is our answer to Macca's Big Mac." Alyne showed some Straya pride.

"Macca's? You mean, MacDonald's?" He shook his head at Alyne. "Extreme Australia..."

At Alyne's recommendation, Cross settled on the Steak and Peppercorn Pie while she ended up with the Minced Beef with Tomato Chutney. Alyne's Pie was decorated with a classic smile, while Cross's had an s-shaped smirk.

"Your Pie looks happier than mine," Cross said,

holding the exit door for Alyne.

"What does that tell you about yourself?" Alyne teased as they continued down Macquarie street.

"Hey, it's my first Pie Face. Go easy on me." Ethan smiled at Alyne's playful banter as he stepped out of the venue onto the sidewalk.

"Oh! You're going to need a drink. Carry on. I'll catch up to you in the Botanical Garden" She pointed across the street. "Some good views of the Opera House for you from there. Ice Coffee, ok?"

"Yes, thank you. Black."

"Ok. No. You're getting a proper Straya ice coffee." Cross watched Alyne hurry back into the Pie Face shop. She was a gracious hostess. Her excitement to show off her city was infectious.

Alyne ordered two ice coffees. She waited for her order to be filled. Behind her, she overheard another waiting-woman speaking loudly into her comm-band. She wore a stylish black and white pencil skirt and posh white wide-rimmed woven sun hat. She paced as she spoke.

"No, I'll be here in Sydney through Monday. I'm making some arrangements for the island. I have someone to meet today to shore up the deal in Brisbane."

Alyne watched the minutes pass on her comm-band as the woman behind her carried on loudly.

"I have another appointment here Monday morning to ensure the supdomene shipment is loaded onto the ship. It shouldn't take long before I can be on my way to join you in Brisbane."

The drinks finally arrived. The barista had added the ice cream scoops that were signature additions to ice coffee in Straya. She was excited to present Cross with his first proper ice coffee experience. Alyne turned quickly as the woman behind her took a pace into Alyne's exit path.

Coffee and ice cream flew onto the woman's stylish garment and dripped to the floor. The stunned woman ended her call abruptly. "Fortinbras, I'll call you back." She directed her anger at Alyne. "You, Barmy Chav. Are you dead from the neck up?" The British woman cursed in French under her breath as she knelt to wipe her skirt. "Tête de noeud."

"I'm so sorry," Alyne knelt as well to help. She glimpsed the woman's wide silver bangle. It had a green jewel inset in the center. "I didn't see you there. My sincere apologies. Let me help."

"You've helped quite enough. Va te faire voir." The black-haired woman dismissed Alyne with a hand.

Alyne felt awful. She stepped away, wishing she could

help. *Strange,* Alyne thought, for a woman with a British accent to hurl French insults. The black-haired woman dismissed a Pie Face employee who had come to her aid. The barista turned to Alyne and offered to make another set of drinks.

In the Botanical Gardens, Cross sat waiting. He had finished a quick call with his old friend in Brisbane, confirming that he and Alyne would meet him and his wife for lunch tomorrow. Cross had parked himself on a bench, drinking in a view of the famous port. He could see sailboats and the light-blue profile of a cruise liner berthed at Circle Quay through the trees. The iconic harbor bridge spanned wide across the harbor above and beyond the opera house's pearl-colored peaks. The landmark was mainly obscured by a canopy of fig branches in the foreground. It was hot. Cross was eager for Alyne to arrive with the refreshments. Soon they could approach the venue together for a clearer view.

With his comm-specs, Cross passed the time searching for a few Sherlock factoids and quotes he might be able to use to impress Alyne. A horoscope about the upcoming solar eclipse was at the top of his email queue. It was from Ila. It read:

Flaws in the essential systems in our lives are revealed around the time of the eclipse, prompting us to redo or to start fresh. Something ends in order for something else to start anew. Although the "new" may be unrecognizable, it is important to allow the necessary surrender to the unknown. Pay attention to the silent people in your life. Often they possess the key to hidden details.

What!? Cross dismissed the spam, baffled by how some people genuinely believe the motion of the stars can affect their lives.

Across the park, a man peered toward Cross through darkly shaded sunglasses. His gaze was directed, not on the stately scene, but rather at the bench where Cross sat with his black and orange backpack to his side. Where was Alyne? Cross checked the time. He decided to phone Logan.

"Logan Kraft's office," Christine's soft voice filled his ear, transmitted from the ear stay of his comm-specs.

"Hello Christine, it's Ethan Cross. Is Logan available?" Cross asked to speak to his mentor.

"You're in luck. He's right here. He doesn't have long before I have him booked, but good timing." Cross heard the rustle of papers as Christine passed the phone to Logan.

"Ethan. How are you? Any new insight?"

Cross cleared his throat. "Not yet, but I'm calling you from Australia, where I just learned from some specialists at Rocket Sci's headquarters that Solcom may be obtaining solar panels from NoviX without proper export licenses. I'm on my way to Brisbane to confirm directly with NoviX."

"Interesting. How are you gaining access to these companies?" Logan inquired.

Cross felt rushed. He hadn't had an opportunity to inform Logan that he was traveling with Alyne, with who he had teamed up since he last spoke to Logan from Kwajielen. "I'm traveling with an associate from Rocket Sci. She shares an interest in getting to the bottom of the export compliance of the solar panels."

"An associate?" Cross could feel Logan smiling. Cross heard Christine hurrying Logan off the call in the background. "Be careful. You know what happened the last time you associated with a foreign lady." Logan referred to Cross' London escapade with a slight chuckle. "By the way, that meeting, the one I mentioned when we last spoke, the out brief triggered by your ARCELOR report; it's moving up. It'll be next month vs. two months out. I'll need you back here shortly after your gallivanting down under. You should still have time to take that R&R I robbed you of in Dubai, but hurry back. Christine is badgering me to go. I hope you unlock the Solcom mystery."

"Me too. Thank you. Goodbye." Cross signed off.
"Good luck Cross, but you won't need luck." Logan was gone.

The voyeur looked on unnoticed by Cross. The figure silently watched, patiently waiting. He reached for the photo button on the ear stay of his comm-specs. The head of a dragon tattoo was visible on his wrist as his sleeve pulled back from the reach. The Polynesian snapped a series of photos of his subject and transmitted them to his employer.

Alyne appeared with an Australian ice coffee topped with an ice cream scoop after a long while. A delicate dusting of cocoa powder decorated the top.

"Sorry for the wait. I had a little run-in with the Wicked Witch of the West. I spilled your first drink order all over her skirt. She was not pleased with me."

"What happened?"

"I turned too fast and walked right into her. It was my fault. And boy, did she let me know it. I received insults in British and French" Cross suppressed a memory of Sirena, an English woman fluent in French that he used to know. The world isn't that small, thought Cross. Logan's reminder of his time in London had put her at the forefront of his thoughts.

"Sorry to hear that. It looks like you made it out unscathed." Cross stole a tall glance of her attractive figure. "Ice cream? Now I know why you thought the rocket looked like an iced coffee. Looks delicious. Thank you"

They continued to the Opera House, walking through the Botanical Gardens parallel to Macquarie Street. Finally, the Opera House was in plain view. Cross framed a photo with his comm-specs of the famous sails on the right, the arch of the Harbor Bridge in the center, and on the left, a massive, elegant turquoise cruise ship docked across the harbor at Circle Quay. On its bow in giant scripted letters, Cross read the words PANACEA. Alyne motioned to the vessel.

"Ever been on a Panacea cruise?"

Cross raised his comm-specs. "That's a long story."

"Seems like you are full of those. Don't you owe me an explanation of your Sherlock Holmes adventure in London? The business trip you mentioned in Dubai?"

"Yes, I do. And don't you owe me the story of how you kick boxed your way out of a meeting?"

"Touché, I can explain when we get to Coogee. Have you had enough of the Opera?" Alyne punched his arm playfully.

The shaded observer watched from up the hill at the edge of the botanical garden through his comm-specs. The partners boarded a hybrid bus bound for the nearby coast. As he watched them depart, a woman in a black and white pencil skirt approached him from behind. She stood at his side, gazing straight ahead at the harbor. The hot Australian sun worked on baking the ice coffee stain from the front of her pencil skirt. She addressed the man in the dark sunglasses without looking his way.

"Your employer and I share an interest in NoviX. Your reports have been most insightful."

The Polynesian nodded.

"The information you provided portraying the questionable nature of their dealings with your employer should help our interests. Armed with your information and the proper context, I suspect my organization will have no concern with the transaction planned for Monday?"

The bald head nodded to concur.

"I thought this meeting would be our final encounter, but there is another matter that has come to light. I received the photo you sent of the duo investigating your employer. The man in the picture, the man you believe knows too much about Solcom's dealings with NoviX, his name is Ethan Cross, and he possesses information sensitive to our pursuits as well."

From behind dark shades, the man's face showed no expression to the woman.

"Our organizations may see a different future for NoviX, but it seems your employer and I are not at odds on the future of Mr. Cross. We cannot have him interfere with our plans on Pitcairn. I don't have to tell you that if he is allowed to share what he knows, it may jeopardize both our interests."

The bald man squared off to the woman, touched the tips of his fingers together, and nodded in a bow of acknowledgment. He said nothing. He possessed more knowledge than both of his employers. The man leaned toward the woman who had paid for access to his confidential corporate information, revealing the fine detail of a tattoo under his sleeves. The artwork depicted a dragon's head wrapped around his wrist, inscribed above Latin text:

In girum imus nocte et consumimur igni

| Chapter 11 |

Red Flags

The aged electric-hybrid bus deposited the explorers at Coogee Beach. The relic struck Cross as an overly complicated machine for a job that a fully electric bus could do. Sydney was behind the times in upgrading its public transportation.

Cross drank in a view of the vast stretch of sand. He saw a group of shirtless Bruces tossing a rugby ball in an awkward underhanded motion. They swung both arms between their legs in a ready position squat and hurled an oblong ball that looked to Cross like a blunt football in a semi-spiral at each other. Nearby, two teams of Sheilas in bikinis stood off against each other on either side of a nearby volleyball net. Cross remarked that all the men and women in Australia seemed fit for a Sports Illustrated magazine. Everyone was attractive here. Alyne was no exception. She held her tailored suit coat under her arm, revealing a short-sleeved tight-fitting undershirt. Cross held his sports coat over his shoulder. It was hot, but a cool breeze was blowing in from over the ocean.

"Not a bad day at the office." Cross stated, "and we didn't have to kickbox our way out of that meeting to get here. So what's your story?"

"My part-time job at Uni before Rocket Sci was a trainer at a kickboxing gym." Alyne started.

"Impressive. You're a kickboxing instructor?" Cross asked.

"Was. Not anymore. I had a client who refused to pay for a week's worth of lessons. He was a traditional boxer and wasn't picking up on the kickboxing technique; he said it was my fault and demanded another lesson. He blocked the door. I had to put him down just to get out."

"You kicked him in the shins?"

"Naw, Yeah, in the face!"

"Extreme Australia," Cross responded.

"Your turn," Alyne said, "What kind of mystery did you solve in London, Dr. Watson? Any truth to what you mentioned in Dubai?"

"Ok, I thought I was Sherlock?"

"You have to tell the story, so you're Watson now. There's time while we walk to Bondi. It's the most famous ocean walk in all of Straya. How's about dinner in Bondi? Roo burgers!" Alyne led the pair to the path that started at the beach's north end. As they left the sandy horseshoe of Coogee, the coastal terrain dramatically changed. The pathway was carved from wind-blown rock. Colorful layers of strata teased untold stories locked in the sediment. Waves crashed below them, slowly eroding the shoreline with the relentless rhythmic cadence, slowly revealing the history of eras gone by. The landscape was beautiful.

"Ok, where to start...." Cross stated out loud, more for himself than for Alyne. He thought he could tell the story short of revealing the Top Secret element. In London, Cross had uncovered that a corporation called EV3 has been building a secretive energy source for over three decades. They called it the ARCELOR. He didn't have to reveal what he discovered, but he could describe how.

"You said you had to escape a dungeon and evade the clutches of an evil corporate mastermind. Start there." Alyne prompted.

"Yes, well, there is a lot to unpack there. That mastermind, his name was Nathan Cain. He was CEO of a company called EV3, and he was like Moriarty. He had thought of every angle and almost caught me."

"Caught you? Why was he chasing you?" Alyne asked the obvious question.

"Let's just say I learned more than he wanted me to know about a product his company manufactured. He detained me in an attempt to control the flow of information, but I escaped."

"Escaped? Do tell."

"Cain, er, Moriarty locked me in an old storage chamber with a woman. I escaped with her help. After some attempted misdirection, I evaded capture."

"Ok- the woman- let's call her Irene Adler." Alyne gave a Sherlock-themed name to the character in Cross' story.

"Irene Adler? You're into this Sherlock parallel, huh?"

"The woman. She's Holmes' love interest in Conan Doyle's original stories."

"Well then, I guess I have some Holmes work to do." Cross flashed a blue-eyed smile to accompany his pun. Alyne smiled back.

"Dad joke." She teased him.

"It wasn't that bad," countered Cross.

"Oh, I didn't say bad, I said, Dad. That was an old man, Dad joke, but now that you mention it...." Alyne teased him with a punch to his arm.

"Ok," Alyne summarized. "Adler and Moriarty chased you across London? Didn't you say that in Dubai? What was that about?"

"I dashed out of there with them in hot pursuit." Ethan could see she was listening intently. "I took the train until they caught up to me at the next train stop. I shook the first set of pursuers at a tower in the Olympic park, but I picked up a second tail. A military drone called a CENTURI."

"Oh, I've seen those in the news. Those are the American police drones. They sent those to Athen's last year, right? There was a crash, I remember."

"Yes. The cause of that crash was what I was in London to investigate. Anyway, long story short, I took the Tube underground to escape the drone. Then I realized it was tracking me. To evade it, I had to ditch my comm-band, which is why I wear this now." He showed off his handsome turquoise timepiece.

"Wow. And you call me Extreme? What was it that you discovered that was so important for them to chase you out of England?"

"If I tell you that, I'd have to kill you." Cross joked, using the cliché phrase to defer answering.

"You're a regular international man of mystery, then aren't you, Mr. Cross?" She matched his platitude. "I'm afraid our quest to NoviX won't measure up. Nonetheless, this solar panel on the interior of a rocket aeroshell is holding my interest, though."

"Agreed. It's a mystery to me. I can't square why Solcom would recover them so far out in the ocean. What could they be being used for after dark?"

"The coordinates you copied from the code, where are they again?"

"They are North West of here, hundreds of miles off shore, deep in the Coral Sea." Cross pointed far over the horizon. Cross thought for a moment. "You know, as far out as the coordinates are from the land, the time zone in the code was the same as the one we're in. Where ever their final location is, they are set up to operate in this time zone. What cities in Australia share our time of day?"

"All the cities on the east coast, I'm afraid. Melbourne, Syndey, Brisbane. Did the code seem to have any mention of day light savings time?" Alyne asked.

"No. I don't believe so."

"Then you can rule out any location south of Queensland. Sydney and Melbourne observe daylight savings time from Spring to Fall. Everything North of Brisbane remains in Australian Standard time year-round."

"Interesting. I guess that helps narrow it down, but it doesn't rule out that the fairings are being used anywhere else in the timezone, like Papa New Guinea or north of there. That's still a lot of possibilities." Cross glanced at the map on his watch for reference. It was afternoon, and he was getting hungry.

"Do you think there's some lost island out there in the Coral Sea? An Island where the fairings are coming down?"

"An uncharted island? You mean like the mystical Skull Island, where King Kong is supposed to live?" He smiled at the idea. "Probably not; I don't think there are any unknown lands left on the planet. Although discovering a mystery island would top my list of bizarre business trip stories." Cross laughed off the idea as his thoughts flashed to Doctor Dodge and his quest to contact another lost island, a silent key, far from the Coral Sea.

"What about that bit where the solar panels receive data at night?" Alyne changed the topic.

Cross had been pondering that himself since he left Dr. Dodge in Kwaj. He had wondered how any signal the panel's tiny nano-scale antennas could detect from ultraviolet to infrared could be strong enough to be pulled out of the background noise. He offered her his leading theory. "They may be receiving information transmitted by light, but I'm still working on how or why."

"Information transmitted by light?" Alyne processed Cross' thought.

"Yes, light. Light of a specific frequency, most likely." Cross thought about the parallel to radio waves that Dr. Dodge had made on Kwaj. Each tiny antenna in the solar panel was sized to the proper length for the receive signals or a frequency of light somewhere between infrared and ultraviolet, but what frequency? A radio could be tuned to receive specific frequencies, sometimes called stations or channels like the shortwave HAM antenna's on the top of Doctor Dodge's Ghost ship. Cross hadn't observed much tuning or filtering circuitry during his short time with the panels, though, so he reasoned that whatever they might be optimized to receive was set with some apriori knowledge of the transmit frequency. Cross knew of only one device that could transmit in the nanoscale wavelength range at a specific frequency. That device was a laser. If the panels were being used as a receiver, the tiny carbon nanotube antennas would respond to various frequencies in the UV, Visible, or IR bands; but what frequency? A signal sent from where to where? And what for, Cross hadn't worked out.

Alyne broke his concentration, "Like the aviation light gun signal? We use those to communicate to planes approaching our safety exclusion zone over Hawke's bay during a countdown. When we can't hail them via radio, we shine an alternating green and red flashing signal from the control tower to tell them to exercise extreme caution." She had offered an unexpected analogy. Lasers weren't on her mind. Her analogy was more like a light house using morse code.

"Ha, you mean like, one if by land, two if by sea?" Cross chuckled, thinking of the famous light signal of American revolutionary war fame. He opted for the playful response versus explaining that a laser signal would have modulation to encode the data that would be significantly more complex than flashing lights.

"Two if by sea? To what are you referring?" Alyne asked.

"Paul Revere?" Cross realized Alyne may not be familiar with the US history trivia, "Nevermind."

"We'll keep thinking about it, Dr. Watson. When you have eliminated the impossible, whatever remains, however improbable, must be the truth." Alyne smiled at her well-placed remark.

"Elementary, my dear Jimmie, elementary." Cross flashed his signature blue-eyed wink.

"Ok, now you can be Holmes again until we sus it out," Alyne returned the Sherlock title to Cross. "Thanks for the John Dory" Cross turned to look at her; an unspoken question lined his face. "The Story," she clarified her Aussie slang.

The pair enjoyed the rest of the walk toward Bondi as they passed more layers of fragmented eons exposed by the walkway excavated from the coastline by the unrelenting waves. The surf's rhythmic crash on the rocky terrain was a pleasant backdrop for their hike. Cross thought it would be an ideal path for a morning run.

"We're almost there. That's Icebergs up ahead. The

Bondi Icebergs Swim Club is at the southern end of Bondi Beach," Alyne stated.

A building with glass windows was perched on the sea below the walkway up ahead. Cross could see two pools of water built behind a low wall separating the square blue-green water from the ocean as they approached. Cross could see a game of Water Polo was in session. It was another foreign sport Cross didn't understand. He looked on with curiosity as they passed. Alyne offered an interesting fact.

"The sea fills the pool. That's why the water is that marvelous blue-green color."

Cross offered some trivia of his own. "The ocean is blue because water absorbs colors in the red part of the light spectrum, which leaves behind colors in the blue part of the light spectrum for us to see. Blue light travels best through the water."

"That, Ethan, is an oddly specific piece of information," she teased.

"You know my method, Dr. Watson. It is founded upon the observation of trifles," Cross quoted Sherlock, hoping to impress her.

"You do know your Holmes, Mr. Cross." She smiled his way. Cross winked proudly.

The off-duty detectives rounded the final curve in the

shoreline walk. Ahead of them, the strata peeled away to reveal a half-mile crescent-shaped expanse of sand and waves. Cross could see surfers decorating the curls on the north side of the beach as Cross and Alyne descended from the low southern hill. A group of four men was tossing a Frisbee beyond a pair of red flags with yellow bottoms. The flag was set in the sand a few hundred feet apart from another red and yellow flag. Swimmers splashed in the water between the markers. Alyne pointed at the surfers.

"Bondi. It's Aboriginal for Surf."

"What are those red flags for?" Cross asked Alyne.

"That's where it's safe to swim," Alyne said matter-of-factly

"And outside the flags? Is it dangerous?" Cross asked.

Alyne laughed at the question. "Depends on what you call dangcrous. Backpackers Express, a curl, is outside the flags, to the north. Lots of people surf there. The southern end of Bondi has a rip tide that can pull you into the Pacific Ocean. Almost all Bondi rescues are in the south and in the afternoon when the tide is shifting."

"So stay between the flags. Keep to the north. It doesn't sound too bad."

"Before noon, they'll have the flags moved south so you can swim there too. There are nets under the water to keep the sharks out of the bay."

"Ok. That's not filling me with confidence. Do the nets work?"

Alyne laughed. "They work just fine. They're baited to attract the sharks so they can be caught and either killed or released."

"Baited. Got it. Attract the sharks to protect the swimmers. Right." Cross restated with sarcasm.

"Relax, Mr. Cross. It's not that dodgy. No one has done the Harry Holt in a while. You should worry about the Irukandji more than the sharks."

"Irukandji?" Cross tilted his head.

"Irukandji jellyfish. They are silent, mysterious, and nearly invisible. They are about 2 centimeters in size and are found in the seas off northern Australia. They can fire their stingers into their victim, causing excruciating pain, cardiac arrest, and death."

"Ah, ok, and what do you have to protect against those?"

"We have the red flags," Alyne stated, pointing at the markers.

Wide-eyed, Cross responded, "Extreme Australia," smiling at Alyne.

The pair of explorers stepped off Nottis Avenue and continued their walk toward the north end of the beach along the grass that lined Campbells Parade, where electric UTEs carrying surfboards sailed by silently. They strolled past a sign that read no-dogs allowed, where a man in surf gear and sandals waited as his small pug relieved itself on the post. Cross and Alyne shared a smile as they both acknowledged the scene's irony.

They continued through the southerly patch of grass bordering the celebrated sand as Alyne took a moment to describe her hometown beach.

"Bondi might be the surf-wear capital of the world." Alyne motioned back to the man and his rebel pug. "Every evening, many drunk wave chasers casually dressed in Roxy, Ripcurl, or Billabong stagger around Campbell Parade. It is a schlep to get to on public transportation; the traffic is a pain; finding a charging dock to park is impossible. But I love that every third restaurant or so is a pizza place and that residents are forever leaving their junk on the sidewalk; designated council clean-up days be damned. I love the apartment blocks weathered by salty air, aspiring musicians, and earnest guitarists leaking music into the street and, never far away, tourists gaping at the views. Every floor of every boutique, fast food seller, and nightclub, however well-intentioned, eventually surrenders to the beach sand on which the suburb is built. Bondi is a disaster if you look closely, but it's my disaster. It's just what a beach should be, with sweet, criminal dogs; cold beers; deep, bright blue water; and parties all night." She beamed about her quirky slice of the Pacific waterfront.

Wow, thought Cross. Her passion for this place was infectious. He wanted to share his hometown with her. He was enjoying his adventure with her. He didn't want it to end. He wondered if she felt the same. He was searching for a sign that she might share his romantic interest. She was spending her weekend with him, which was a positive sign, but then again, she had been more familiar with Rick in Dubai, *hadn't she?*

"Aren't you from Melbourn? You talk like you grew up here in Bondi."

"Righto, I live there now, but I went to Uni here in Sydney, and you?" Alyne volleyed his question back at him with genuine interest. That's a positive sign, he thought.

"College? Harvard in Boston." He cringed inwardly, awaiting one of the usual stereotypical reactions. Would it be a comment suggesting he came from a wealthy background? Would she feign a remark about his smarts? Or razz him about being admitted through nepotism? He prepared to counter any of these typical cliches, but none came. Instead, Alyne pointed to their left and reminded Cross.

"It's time for your roo burger."

They approached a rotary at the corner of a skate

park and some vacant electric car chargers along the drive that met the sand. A small venue with a neon sign that read Roo Bangas was tucked between two larger buildings overlooking the horseshoe of sand.

"Roo burger? As in Kangaroo?"

"Bloody Oath. You can pay a lot for a cut cooked medium with a side of beats and rockets, but it's best between a bikky." Alyne explained with excitement.

"Rockets? What's that?" Cross asked. "Sounds like something you'd like."

"Too Right. Rockets are lettuce in the States. Arugula leaves, I think you call it?"

They ordered takeout from Roo Bangas and exited facing the ocean. They sat on the grass patch just past the skate park and ate as they watched the disk players launch a Frisbee from a perfect view of the most famous strip of sand in the world. Their shadows reached long toward the ocean as the sunset at their back. The roo burger tasted like lean beef to Cross. The rockets added a tartness that paired perfectly with the flavor. It was delicious. Alyne pointed at the disc players on the beach ahead of them. "You ever play flying disk?"

"Frisbee? Yes," Cross replied.

Alyne stood, left her suit coat on the grass, and approached the men. Cross followed, leaving his sports coat over his backpack. She put her hand up without a word, and the players tossed her the disk. Cross stepped back to increase the distance between himself and where Alyne stood. She passed him a level toss. Cross caught it and spun the Frisbee to the next player standing at the edge of the sea. The man stood as far from Cross as Cross felt he could throw the Frisbee. He observed the other men were standing significantly farther apart. He and Alyne were standing closer to each other than the other players. Cross stood as far from the man at the wave break as possible while retaining his ability to reach the player with his most decisive toss.

Hundreds of feet away, a shadowy figure emerged from Roo Bangas. He gazed through dark comm-specs at the flying disk game occurring on sands of Bondi ahead in the distance. He raised his arm to reach the photo button on the ear stay of his eyewear. The sleeve of his shirt slipped back, offering a partial glimpse at the ornate dragon artwork etched into his skin. He snapped a series of pictures and perched himself where he could patiently watch the match run its course.

The Frisbee continued around the circle counterclockwise from player to player until the sunset was too low, and it was too dark to continue the game. Cross admired that the group with the disk had been so accepting of two randos joining their match. The players came together to greet the strangers who had invited themselves into their game. The first of the men to reach Cross and Alyne beckoned for the others to hurry up. He seemed to be in charge.

"G'day. I'm Cap. I've gotta say now that we are within cooee, you've got a strong arm on ya." The first tall shirtless Aussie said to Cross. Cap turned to Alyne, "I was a stunned mullet to see you two-stepping to play all snowed under." The captain motioned to her business attire. They were wearing considerably more clothes than the players. The Aussie continued, "You're all rugged up to go to the retro party?" The man asked as another player reached earshot.

"That was a ripsnorter." The second man stated as he came to a stop and stuck out his hand. "Nothing wonky from you two." He looked at Cross, "Your toss is sweet as a Lamington. You gonna join us at the club?"

"Ethan Cross." Cross shook the second man's hand and nodded as the two others arrived. He observed, "You guys were standing pretty far apart from each other. It was all I could do to reach you with the Frisbee."

The team captain responded to the observation. "Think nothing of it, Mate. We're on the Australian National Ultimate team. Good on you to hold your own with us." He said in a friendly tone.

"Do you mean a professional Ultimate Frisbee team?"

"Naw, Yeah, Frisbee. Flying disk, but yeah. We're heading to Hotel Ravesis." He pointed directly behind them at the two-story white building on the corner of Campbell Parade and Hall Street. "You two should join us. We have a table."

"The retro party? You have a private table?" Alyne asked.

"Strewth. They have an early 2000's retro music party. Mates Rates."

Alyne looked at Cross for a signal. "You in?"

Cross fired back enthusiastically. "I'm in."

Cross picked up his coat and backpack from the edge of the grass as they approached the Hotel Ravesis nightclub with their newfound friends.

A short line was forming at the venue's entrance. Cross and Alyne followed the team, who was granted preferential access. The Ulitmate Captain glanced back at Cross and Alyne and said,

"These two Nipper Grommet's are with us for a drinkee. It's my shout."

Cross laughed and remarked to Alyne so only she could hear, "Why you Aussies gotta abrev ev'thing?"
She smiled as the bouncer allowed Alyne and Cross to pass by association with the semi-celebs.

As they passed into the nightclub entrance, a bald man wearing sunglasses stepped from the shadows to the end of the line and waited outside to enter.

| Chapter 12 |

Drinkee

Cross could see that the venue had been transformed from a restaurant by day to a nightclub at sunset as they entered the dark room. The Ultimate team led them to a round table on an elevated terrace with a circular booth of leather seating enclosing most of the table's perimeter. The private table's open quarter faced a busy dance floor sunken below the ground level. Alyne followed Cross into the club.

"Cross," Alyne shouted over the song that was ending. "Cross, look, the handle of your pack lights up in the blacklight." She spoke loudly to draw his attention to the orange rubber lift handle on the top of his black sack. Cross slipped it off of one shoulder to see for himself. Sure enough, its grip phosphoresced iridescently like the bioluminescent glow worms in the caves of New Zealand.

"Oh, that's wild." Cross acknowledged Alyne's observation over the loud music. He knew that some materials absorb ultraviolet light and re-emit it almost instantaneously. The emitted visible light has a longer wavelength than the shorter UV radiation it absorbed, making the light visible and causing the material to glow like biolume. Cross stole a glance at Alyne's neckline. The white shirt under her tailored suit coat was glowing like the handle of Cross' backpack.

"You're glowing too!" Cross pointed at her chest.

"Oh, wow!" Alyne shouted, removing the overcoat of her casual business attire. She looked like an angel in the blacklight. Cross looked beyond her. UV lights lined the ceiling of the dance floor. White t-shirts and bikini tops radiated from a pool of dancers raving below in the low light.

A laser projector emanating from some hidden location in the club beamed the next song's title onto a pane of glass that hung beyond the pit of dancers so all could see. The text floated in the air above the patrons as the 30-year-old song began to play.

Sofi Tukker- Drinkee, 2017 Grammy nominee for Best Dance Recording.

The vintage music started as Cross, Alyne, and the team took their seats. Cross slipped his backpack off and slid it along the curved leather bench seat to his side as he shifted his way around the table. The Ultimate Captain ordered a bottle for the team. The song's unique sound of cowbells and bongos proceeded as an electric guitar riff mixed over the beat.

The liquor was delivered promptly and was set in the center of the table. It was served in a bucket of ice that glowed blue, lit from beneath. The server slid shot glasses, illuminated by a mesmerizing blue across the table to each party member. The team leaned in for the

Captain's toast as the female vocalist sang nonsensical Portuguese lyrics amid deep driving bass. He shouted.

"We love the ones that do!
We like the ones that don't!
We hate the ones that say they will
But then they say they won't!"

The Captain addressed Cross with a smile to finish the toast. The song's lyricist sang the word *Drinkee* as if on cue.

"But the Sheila's we like most of all,
And I know you'll think I'm right.

Are Sheila's who say, I never will!
But just for you, I might!"

The team cheered, downed the blue concoction, and stood. Organized chaos ensued as the Captain led the team to the dance floor. Cross and Alyne shared an empty booth. For a fleeting moment, their gazes locked. Alyne leaned forward. In that instant, Cross thought it might be a signal inviting a kiss. He tipped his body toward her just as her lean transformed into a stand as she rose to follow the foreign sports team to the dance floor. She grabbed Cross' hand, looking back with a smile as she pulled him toward the raving surf. *What was that?* Cross thought of the brief encounter with measured excitement.

A series of small drones with colorful lights deployed

from the ceiling above. They were shaped like tiny flying doughnuts. Small central lift motors acted as fans, cooling the dancers below. The lights flashed to the music's beat as they moved to the foreign melody in coordinated unison out of reach overhead. The colors alternated in a mesmerizing rhythmic fade. The small indoor formation moved counter-clockwise, drawing party-goers' attention as they danced below. Alyne's gaze dropped from above and met Cross'. Cross reached for her hand, and they shared a smile as they moved to the rhythm.

The song reached a bridge of slow, dropping bass and trance sounds. The drop in tempo deprived the starved sun worshipers of the rapid movements they had been compelled to make just moments before. The song's pace commanded a collective lull in the crowd as the flashing lights from the drones overhead slowed. Again, Alyne's eyes met Ethan's. He raised her hand in his over their heads. Alyne broke the lock with a flirty half-spin and backed toward him as she lowered his arm around her waist. Cross briefly glanced over Alyne's shoulder at their table and the blue-lit bottle. He spotted the blue, glowing shot glasses they had used minutes earlier as they swayed together to the rhythm. He saw an orange handle bob in the darkness between flashes of light from the decorative drones. His pack's handle rose above the edge of the table into his view in the hands of a silent bald man.

The Polynesian slipped Cross's pack onto his shoulder. Cross was being robbed! Cross vainly yelled across the room, "Hey!" His shout was muffled by bass and Portuguese babble. "Hey!" he pulled his arm briskly away from Alyne.

He tried to wade his way through the turbulent water of clubbing dancers. The smooth bottoms of his dress shoes struggled for traction on a dance floor covered in sand that years of surfing ravers had carried from Bondi. He fumbled to part the sea as the thief bounded from the table toward the exit with Cross' backpack. Cross could see the glowing handle of the knapsack rushing away from him on the back of the robber. The music picked up pace. The ravers stifled Cross' pursuit. He pushed dancers back, caught in the rip curl of trance. He perceived a shout from Alyne between a dip in the wave of the music. "Hey!"

Cross caught another glimpse of the burglar through the ocean of people. A bald man wearing sunglasses wore his bag. The thief slipped farther away, moving quickly by the edge of the dance pit where Cross struggled to escape like quicksand. The robber passed the bouncer and sped out of the Ravesis Hotel. Cross freed himself and raced to the exit. Alyne shouted over the music, "Cross! Cross!" He burst into the street just in time to see the Polynesian looter fleeing around the block.

"Damn!" The thief escaped with Ethan's luggage. Alyne reached him and demanded an explanation.

"What was that about!?" Alyne stated, out of breath.

"My backpack. It was stolen! Damn it."

"What!? Who would do that?" She asked rhetorically. Cross described the perpetrator. A bald Polynesian man with sunglasses.

"Strange. Do you think we're being followed?"

| Chapter 13 |

Brisbane

"S'Arvo now, ya hungry?" Alyne said to Ethan. The briny seaside odor reminded Ethan of the salty New England seacoast, freshly cooked lobster, and steamed clams. Brisbane was a long way from New England "Chowda," but the dirty ocean river water gave it a familiar friendly feel.

"Am I ever. We're meeting my friend for lunch. We're running a bit late" Ethan checked the turquoise face of his wristwatch, and for that instant, he admired the intricate world map that lay behind the classic hands. The watch was less of a souvenir; it was a scar he had earned in battle, which he wore proudly. He was glad Alyne was more trustworthy than Sirena, the duplicitous woman who had given him the decorative scar. Alyne had been a helpful partner in their quest for answers on the enigmatic rocket solar panels thus far, and he was actually enjoying working the mystery together with someone. Her Holmes-Watson banter had been enjoyable. *Maybe he could work with a partner after all?* Cross thought again of Sirena and London and considered his own thought. *The right partner.*

They stepped together off the odd asymmetrical work

of architecture called the Goodwill pedestrian bridge. They continued their stroll along the scenic Brisbane River walkway approaching the Clem Jones Promenade on the river's south bank. They were five miles inland from Moreton Bay, but they could still feel the ocean brush through their hair. The riverside trail was bustling with activity. Rollerbladers, joggers, and dog walkers crossed paths all around them. A few small signs they had passed along the way let them know they were approaching a public pool.

"Sorry about your pack getting lifted last night." Alyne offered, "You think someone was after your lappy? A rival defense contractor?"

"My comm-pad? I doubt it was anyone in defense or even in espionage. Most people in the industry know that American contractors don't travel with tech data. People in the community are aware that biometric access and encryption are so much better than commercial anti-tamper measures that cyber theft would not be worth the effort. You'd have to be, or think you were, a savant in information technologies to have a shot at hacking a DoD comm-pad. I figure it was just a random thief. Probably a broke Bondi musician."

"Deadset, I recon." Alyne continued, "You're right. It was a crook, Fair Dinkum."

"Yeah." Cross trailed off. It would be an inconvenience. The thief had made off with his bathing suit, some clothing, and his comm-pad. It would be the second piece of company computing equipment he'd have to report stolen in as many business trips. Logan and Christine would not be impressed. At least he still had his comm-specs, and the business attire from last night would be formal enough for their upcoming visit to NoviX. He reminded himself that the loss might all be worth it if they came away from their meeting at NoviX with some answers about the rocket fairings and their ultimate application.

Alyne could see he was brooding and changed the subject to something more pleasant, "Ever been to Melbourne? I've always likened this skip along the Brisbane River to a walkabout the Yarra. It's similar to the public beach walk at Birrarung Marr." Ethan had never been to Melbourne, but the river walk reminded him of his hometown. "I was thinking it was similar to walking along the Chaz on a summer day in Beantown." Beyond a row of palm trees, a throng of paddle boarders enjoyed the warm, clean river air. There were no other boats on this stretch of the river beyond the pedestrian bridge they had crossed.

"Beantown? The Chaz? You have a funny way of speaking." Alyne laughed.

"That's funny. I was thinking the same thing." Ethan smiled back.

Cross dropped his comm-specs down over his eyes and focused his view about three-quarters of a mile upstream in the direction they were headed. Victoria

Bridge crossed low above the water, explaining why he saw no sailboats. On a day like today along the Charles, he would expect to see sailfish and crew boats all about. No quad sculls or sweeping boats were feathering and squaring their way upstream either. He thought Crew boats would have no trouble rowing below the low bridges. Only the group of paddleboarders was out to enjoy the river. The calm water reminded him he was thirsty from the heat.

What's your mate's name again, Bling?" Alyne asked.

"Jay Blah," Ethan smirked, recalling the occasion when his friend had earned the moniker "Blah." It was coined by a pair of lap-legged sorority sisters making a Virginia fence at a frat party who couldn't enunciate his full name.

"Blah, what nationality is that?" Alyne asked.

"He's Puerto Rican. His real name is Jovanie Louise Zayas something, something. No one can remember or pronounce his full name, so he goes by Blah."

"That's Dardy. Where are we meet'n him?"

"Jay and his wife are waiting for us at the Plough Inn; it should be close."

"I know it, chuck a blocky after the lagoon."

"Chuck a blocky?" Ethan smiled at her alluring Aussie

slang.

"Naw Yeah, bang a U-ie. This way."

Alyne pointed ahead to where the pedestrian path curved away from the river—beyond a sizeable public pool on their left, separated from the river by their pathway. The landlocked pool looked more like an inland sliver of ocean beach than a community water park. It was complete with palm trees and kids in colorful bathers making sandcastles. The white sand was decorated with sharp-looking shirtless Bruces and bikini-clad Shelias worthy of a rubber neck. Alyne led the way along a pathway between the Brisbane River pool Lagoon and a smaller adjacent pool.

Ethan recognized Jay Blah's laugh from the street as he and Alyne approached the Plough Inn straight ahead of them.

"That's it." Alyne pointed to the two-story establishment directly ahead. Jay Blah and his wife sat at an outdoor table on the second-story porch deck. Ethan figured that they had been seated for an hour, probably had had their lunch, and were enjoying another cocktail. Ethan fondly recalled that Jay's volume increased as he got pixilated.

"I figured that was the place." Ethan smiled as they neared the venue's street-side facade. They entered the establishment, informed the polite, slim hostess that they were meeting guests. The mildly attractive server escorted them to where Jay and his wife were sitting. Ethan spoke first as he arrived at a long table along the rail where Jay held the head seat.

"Freakin' 'Rican. How 'you been?"

"Ethan Cross, you old coxswain, you. Good place to get Ploughed, don't you think?" Jay stood to greet the visitors, gesturing wide, armed at the river's grand view over the public pool lagoon. "Please sit down."

Ethan introduced his companion, "This is Alyne Jimmie of Rocket Sci."

"Glad to meet you. This is my better half, Kelsy."

"G' day." Jay's wife stood at her seat and offered her hand to Alyne. "Excuse my husband; he's had heaps of Goon."

Everyone took their seats as Jay asked the tiny waitress for a round of drinks. "Maybe another schooner and some ponies?" He directed his remarks to Ethan and Alyne, "have a feed, as they say here."

"Ponies? You've gone native, have you? We heard you from the street a ways off," Ethan said affectionately as he sat.

"Yeah, Well, I've never been told to speak up, that's for sure," Jay laughed jovially. "There was that one time at a house party in Southie when being loud did me no favors. I found myself at a deaf convention after-party."

Ethan knew Blah's story, but he prompted him to continue, "Is this when you asked out a girl using sign language?" Ethan had first heard the story years ago the following morning after the encounter when he had met up with Jay for a late morning run the next day.

"Well, it went down like this. I had just arrived in town from Worcester. Jarrett, a friend of mine, had talked up this big house party that was going down at a multistory apartment building in the south end. He said there would be multiple kegs, lots of girls, and music. I was in!"

Jay had an engaging way of telling stories. Everyone at the table was leaning forward, ready to enter the kegger with Jay. Even Jay's wife listened intently. Seemingly, the story had never come up at their kitchen table.

"I arrive at the scene, and sure as shit, the apartment was full of people. You could see it was packed from the street. We squeezed our way in to find the keg located on the first story. Immediately, Jarrett was consumed by the crowd. He was nowhere to be found. I was alone. I figured I'd make my way upstairs, hoping to run into him. As I did, two things struck me as odd about this gathering. The lights were full-on, and while Jarrett was right about the kegs, there was no music. It was far too quiet for a mixer of this size." Jay paused to sip from his pony as Ethan and Alyne ordered food. Two roo burgers.

"I reached the top floor—no sign of Jarrett. I didn't know anyone there. I glanced across the apartment into an open concept kitchen area and saw a tall attractive blonde signing hand gestures to a brunette waiving signals back. That explained it! No one at this party could hear. As I learned later, there had been a deaf convention elsewhere in the city that day, and I was at the after-party!" The table shared a round of chuckles, Jay continued, fueled by the laughter.

"Ok, I thought. Beer, check. Girls, check. But I couldn't spend a night partying with no music. I spotted an antique disc player nearby in the corner of the room. It sat on an unstable old coffee table. It had dozens of old CDs scattered around it. I grabbed a vintage 40-year-old disc with the picture of a black rapper in a do-rag and cued up a song titled "In Da Club." I figured this ought to spice things up a bit. The song started at a moderate volume. "Hey Shorty, it's your birthday. We're gonna party like it's your birthday." No one noticed. I turned it up. Loud. CDs and cases started vibrating off the table. No one in the room even flinched; they just kept on signing away to each other as if nothing had changed."

Ethan glanced at Alyne, who was enjoying the story. She was laughing while she took a sip from her afternoon wine. Ethan noticed a commercial airliner passing overhead. Its older style conventional jet engines were faintly audible as it throttled down on its final approach to the Brisbane airport situated at the mouth of the river on the harbor. Jay pulled his attention back to the deaf party in Boston.

"A girl nearby finished a set of hand signals and then turned to someone on her opposite side to speak a few words." Jay continued, "I beelined over to her, 'Excuse me,' I said, 'but I noticed you're not deaf?' 'No,' she shouted over the music, 'I'm a translator.' "A translator?" I said, "that's great! Can you teach me to sign something?" 'Sure,' she said. 'What do you want to learn?' "I don't know," I said."

Jay put his hands out, mimicking his reaction in the moment. His facial expression at the head of the table replicated the confusion of the encounter. "Teach me the words to this song," I said as the song repeated the chorus, "Hey Shorty, it's your birthday, we're gonna party like it's your birthday."

Jay stood, sliding his chair away with the backs of his knees. He started to dance in place at the table, demonstrating the signs for the song's lyrics as he sang them.

"Great," I said. "I've got it! Let's go meet someone, come with me." I said to the translator. I picked the hottest deaf girl I could find. I escorted the translator across the kitchen to the tall blond as the song's chorus began. The rap beat repeated, "Hey Shorty, it's your birthday, we're gonna party like it's your birthday." I pointed at the sexy silent siren and showed her my newly acquired communication skills in rhythm to the song. She tilted her head and looked at me like I was crazy. I get that a lot, I know. I turned to the translator for help. The translator looked up at me and pulled my hand down from the birthday symbol. 'Hey, Hey,' the translator shouted at me, 'She's probably never heard that song.'"

The table of new friends roared with laughter. Even people sitting nearby were chuckling. Jay's wife had snarfed some of her wine in astonishment and amusement. Jay had a way of telling stories, a stage presence that ought to have been put to use acting. He missed his calling. Instead, he was an ex-pat working in the telecom industry as an engineer, or a manager of some sort, Ethan wasn't sure.

"Did she give you the silent treatment after that?" Ethan joked with his friend.

"Haha. She flashed me a single-fingered sign I recognized over the music, that's for sure."

"I tried to recover by quickly asking the translator to change the topic. I said to the translator, ask her if she knows braille? I was about to tell her a funny story about a brail playboy I once read. Instead, the translator looked me straight in the eyes and said, 'braille is for blind people.'"

"Ohh, I didn't *see* that comin'," Ethan was quick with the pun. Jay gave a hearty laugh. The old friends entertained Alyne. It was as if they hadn't been apart for years.

Kelsy interrupted the commiseration offering a mild check to the inanity with a playful glare at her husband, "Have you boys ever considered that silence is the key to paying better attention to details?"

Kelsy's comment cooled the mode. The look on her face reminded the men that were being obtuse. Alyne broke the awkwardness and addressed Jay next, "What do you do for work, Jay?"

Jay lapsed into professionalism, "I'm an operations manager for a telecoms company. We install and maintain internet service to large commercial and industrial clients. The job pays the bills, and for my habit- I mean hobby- down there." Jay pointed at a large coral-colored four-door Cadillac convertible that must have been nearly 80 years old. It had Texas longhorns on the front and exuded a very Cuban or Miami vibe anchored on the street awaiting its skipper.

"Wow," Ethan said, "That's no electric. Where'd you find an old Caddy like that on this continent?"

"I didn't find her here. I had her shipped over on a cable laying ship a few years ago now. She's my other love." Jay reached over to squeeze his wife's hand. He blew her a kiss, and Kelsy rolled her eyes.

"A cable laying ship?" Ethan asked. He'd get back to car talk.

"Yeah, the Caddy came from Guam, actually. I

worked out a deal with our cable carriers to take it here on their last cable-laying expedition. It took months, but it didn't cost much."

"What do you mean cable-laying expedition?" Alyne asked the same question that was on Ethan's mind.

"Brisbane is the landfall site of major undersea cables for Australia. It was almost ten years ago when I first moved to Brisbane for this job. That was the most recent cable drop since the last drop in 2020 that really opened up the internet for Australia. Business has been booming here ever since."

"Opened up the internet in Australia? Can't you get internet via the LEO satellite constellations?" Ethan asked.

"Yes, but nothing beats the speed and reliability of an undersea cable. Fiber-optic submarine cables crisscross the ocean floor worldwide, carrying 95–99% of international data over bundles of fiber-optic fibers, some no larger than the diameter of a garden hose. Besides," Jay concluded, "They haven't figured out how to get a powerful enough transmitter into tiny wearable devices like comm-bands and comm-specs for mobile devices to take much advantage of satellite-based internet." He pointed at Ethan's shades. "No uploading pics to satellites directly from those things."

Fascinating, thought Ethan, recalling the lecture he had received from Doctor Dodge on Kwaj a few days ago.

Funny, he had never given undersea internet cables a thought before, and twice now within the week, the topic had come up.

"What brings you down under?" Jay's Boston accent betrayed the American transplant to the Outback's authenticity.

"We are on a quest to solve a mystery!" Alyne answered for Ethan with a big smile.

"A quest? Sounds exciting. Are we talking about an old-fashioned quest with knights and princesses locked in castle towers? Do you have to fight a dragon at the end?" Jay said jokingly.

"We are on our way to a company called NoviX here in Brisbane. They make a new solar panel that puts out four or five times the traditional cell's energy. It's being used in an unusual application that we are investigating." Ethan sized up the central mystery for Jay.

"Oh, it's more than that," Alyne added with enthusiasm, "the solar panel is a component in the rocket nose cone of a payload that my company launches routinely. We've launched hundreds for a Chinese customer called Solcom. It's an export-controlled technology, and we are trying to find out if they are being supplied legally."

"Hundreds? Doesn't it take a few years to launch hundreds of rockets? Wouldn't the legal questions have come up before now?" Jay posed an insightful question.

"Yes. It gets more interesting, you see, the solar panels are integrated into the inside surface of the rocket nose cone fairing. You can't see that they are solar panels from the exterior." Ethan provided another element of mystery to the case.

"And, as the launch provider, we never see inside the payload. In fact, we only oversee the final integration of the payload to the rocket fuselage for this customer. The customer packages their payload and seals it into the fairing assembly before it gets to Rocket Sci for final stage assembly at our facility on Ahuriri Point in New Zealand." Alyne provided more insight.

"How do you know that there is a solar panel on the inner surface if you never get to see inside?" Jay was gaining interest.

"That's why I'm here," Ethan said. "One of the fairings was recovered in the ocean and taken to a US Army facility. I was called in to investigate."

Jay opened his mouth to follow his line of inquiry.

"And how did you two meet?" Kelsy chimed in before her husband had a chance to ask his next question.

Ethan looked at Alyne. She smiled as Ethan answered, "We met skiing in Dubai."

"Isn't Dubai in the middle of the desert? You can ski there?" Kelsy seemed perplexed.

"Yes. Certainly the most bizarre business trip outing. And what's stranger is later that week, this same bloke arrives at Rocket Sci asking about this fairing." Alyne punched Ethan's arm playfully.

"Why were you in Dubai?" Kelsy continued.

"Wait a minute." Jay interrupted his wife's question to redirect the conversation, "What do you mean, the fairing was recovered in the ocean? You mean by a submarine?"

"No, the fairings float," Ethan added.

"That's wicked weird. So you've seen one up close? What else did you learn about it?" Jay was hooked now.

"Yeah. It appears that they are built to be waterproof. They don't appear to be designed to work in Space. The circuitry indicates that they can generate power like a normal solar cell, but it looks like they can switch into some communications mode. There is circuitry that looks like a radio receiver that switches in. And here's the weird part. It appears that the mode switch occurs at night."

"What? None of that adds up." Jay said. Before he could ask a follow-up question, Alyne spoke up excitedly.

"Oh, Rick is going to join us. He says he'll be here soon." Alyne cast her comm-band keyboard on the white tabletop to respond to the message scrolling across the device on her wrist.

"Rick? Rick Chan?" Ethan asked, surprised, "He knows you are here?" Ethan's guard went up.

"Yes. I've been texting him since we left for Sydney. I asked him if he knew anything about solar panels on his payload."

"You've been texting him since we left Rocket Sci? Why didn't you tell me?" Cross fought to hide his annoyance. Was this girl playing him? What was her game? Maybe he should have trusted his instincts in New Zealand? This was why he preferred to work alone.

"Rick hadn't responded until just now. I thought he would have some information. After all, he is the Chief Technical Officer. If anyone would know about the fairings, it should be him, right?" She glanced back at her comm-band to read more incoming text. Cross watched her suspiciously. Ethan felt alienated. How could he have let himself trust her? He had made that mistake before. "He says he'll be landing in minutes. I'll tell him we're at the Plough Inn." She finished typing her response.

"Well, how did he know you are in Brisbane?" Ethan asked.

"I had sent him another text from Sydney. Here it is."

Alyne tipped her wrist toward Ethan to reveal the outgoing message from yesterday. It read:

Do you know NoviX? Heading to Brisbane to speak with them about supplying Rocket Sci via Solcom.

Cross leaned back, folding his arms over his chest.

"Is he coming just to see you?" After the words left his mouth, Ethan immediately wondered if his question would reveal his romantic interest in Alyne. She didn't appear to pick up on it.

"No, he's got a business meeting here in Brisbane on Monday. He says he was coming here anyway, so he suggested we meet. I should go freshen up. Where's the dunny?" Alyne asked.

"It's over by where you came up the stairs," Kelsy pointed politely. "Here, I'll join you."

The two Aussie women stood together to leave the table. Ethan and Jay watched them make their way to the restroom. Jay spoke first.

"Who is this Rick Chan guy?"

"He's the CTO of a communications company I met in Dubai at the airshow. He's Asian and a bit flamboyant. He's got a lot of money, and he's not afraid to mention it. He seems to know his tech, but he's arrogant and condescending about it." Ethan felt a twinge of competitiveness as he recalled the ski jumping showdown at his last encounter with the man.

"Hmmm," Jay pondered Ethan's response and changed the subject. "And what's the deal with you and Alyne, buddy? She's a knockout. You two...ya know?" Jay raised his eyebrows toward Ethan. "And what's her deal with Rick?"

Ethan took a shot of the wine left in his glass. "It's not like that, and I don't know, but this Rick guy is all over her, you'll see."

"Richard? Not a very Asian name. Richard Chan? He sounds like a real Dick."

Jay and Ethan shared a long laugh. Ethan continued to tell Jay about skiing in Dubai. After a few minutes, the girls returned to the table. Alyne had received another text from Rick.

"Rick texted that he will touch down in a couple of minutes. He said to order him a coldie. Anyone else?" Alyne sat, looking around for the petite server.

"He won't arrive that quickly. It took us nearly an hour to get here from the airport, albeit we opted to walk halfway, but still, a beer won't be cold by the time he arrives." Ethan observed.

As he finished the statement, another jet, a small commuter plane, passed into view from their table following the same final approach path into Brisbane airport that the airliner had taken earlier. Cross' gaze over her shoulder caught Alyne's attention, and she turned to look at the sky above the river. The jet banked left, deviating from the glideslope that would have brought it to rest on the runway five miles away. Instead, it dropped lower and banked again in the opposite direction into a wide sweeping right-hand turn as it descended. It leveled out low over the Victoria Bridge on a trajectory toward the Goodwill pedestrian bridge where they had crossed the river earlier. The aircraft was closer now. It had a distinctive profile that Cross recognized. It was an Intellagama. It was on final approach to land on the Brisbane river right in front of them. Rick Chan was arriving in the world's most coveted status icon.

Jay and Kelsy joined the gazers. Patrons of the lagoon in the foreground of their vantage point began to take note. A few bikini-clad Aussies ran together from the pool to the river's edge for a better look at the sleek white airplane as it kissed the still river water. Its first touch with the water's surface sent a beautiful symmetrical spray of water cleanly in either direction from its boat-shaped bow. For a lingering moment, the mist birthed tiny rainbows that soon faded as the aircraft skipped ahead. It touched the surface again a few meters farther downstream, squarely abeam of the Plough Inn. The plane's sudden arrival caught the group of paddleboarders by surprise. Cross watched them drop to their knees on their boards, clutching them for stability. The river water arrested the airplane's speed as it slowed to a motorboat's pace a few hundred yards short of the

Goodwill Bridge. One unfortunate paddleboarder lost her balance and fell into the river as the plane's wake reached her position near the shore. The aircraft turned and taxi-ed in the direction of the Lagoon and came to a complete stop fifty feet from the riverbank. It stopped in front of the shoreline at Clem Jones Promenade.

The aircraft's rear cargo door hinged open under the high tail wing in no time. A small rowboat-sized skiff emerged. Its single occupant steered the small tender to the shore, manning a wheel that controlled a little built-in electric trolling motor. Rick Chan docked the small boat at the Promenade and traded pleasantries with the onlookers and the bikinis who had chanced to greet him. He briskly strode from the impromptu welcome party like a celebrity entering a premiere. He continued on a vector toward the Plough Inn. Alyne pointed and whispered something to Kelsy. Cross burned with jealousy, and he doused it with a long sip from his fresh coldie.

"Look at this guy," said Jay. "Strolling in like Batman. Who does he think he is? Bruce Wang?" Ethan and Jay shared another belly laugh as Rick passed by Jay's coral Caddy, strode across the street, entered the Inn, and was escorted to their table by the dainty waitress. She armed him with a Saturday afternoon brew as he took a seat at the table by Alyne.

"Rick Chan, Solcom, good to meet y'all" Rick used his semi-Texan speak. The team exchanged greetings.

"That was quite the entrance," stated Cross. "That's the Intellagama, isn't it?" Ethan was interested in the plane, not the man.

"Yes, she's brand new. I picked her up a few days ago in Dubai. She's a marvelous machine." Rick said, beaming.

"It's a beautiful plane." said Jay, "what does Intellagama mean?"

"Intellagama. It's named after an Australian water dragon. It's built by MagiX here in Australia with electric engines from China, speaking of dragons...." Rick looked from Ethan to Alyne and pulled something from his pocket to hand to her. It was a necklace with a short black leather band and an S-shaped pendant carved from green stone with pointy hook-like barbs at either end.

"It's a Pounamu Dragon necklace from New Zealand. It's like no other Maori jade. It is said to dissolve grief and separation. I picked it up in NZ yesterday. As soon as I saw it, I thought of you." He offered the souvenir to Alyne and continued, "In Asian cultures, dragons are angelic, fierce, and benevolent protectors that watch over us. Representing supernatural power and hidden knowledge, they control the world's waters." She thanked him but didn't put it on. Instead, she slipped the heavy stylized pendant and leather strap choker into her pocket. The exchange made Cross seethe. He kept his emotions to himself. This guy was an ass.

"You remember Ethan, don't you, Rick? From skiing in Dubai?" Rick looked at Cross for a moment. "Oh, yes, I thought you looked familiar. You did that cute little rotation on the slopes. We lost track of you shortly after. A coincidence, running into each other again here." Ethan didn't answer before Jay spoke up.

"Solcom, what kind of business are you in, Rick?" Jay said to Chan, defusing some of the tension he knew was plaguing his old friend. Cute rotation, Cross thought? That trick was a helicopter, and it was most certainly not *cute*.

"Solcom is in telecommunications. We have stood up a low earth orbit constellation of satellites I call Icarus. It provides internet worldwide, focusing on the developing market in China. We have the best in class, unmatched download speeds."

"What brings you here to Brisbane?" Cross asked next.

"I have an important business meeting at NoviX on Monday."

"That's where we are headed." Alyne chimed in. "What can you tell us about NoviX supplying to Solcom?"

Rick started with a prepared response. "Yes. I saw your message a few days ago. Your interest in NoviX coincides with my own. I'm headed there to secure an acquisition deal that has been in the works for quite some time."

"Acquisition? What are you ordering from NoviX?" Ethan asked, expecting the answer to include the enigmatic fairings. He thought the question might begin to steer the conversation toward the answers they were seeking.

"No. This meeting is not about ordering. This meeting is about Solcom acquiring NoviX."

"You're buying a whole company? Wow," Ethan stole a glance at Jay. "I'm buying new sneakers," Ethan said. Jay laughed into his drink.

"It's an investment that Solcom has been shaping for several years, and I'm excited that it's finally concluding. Tell me, how is it that you suspect NoviX to be a supplier to Solcom?"

Ethan thought about his response. Where to start? He wondered about Rick's choice of words. Suspect? Why wouldn't he have confirmed NoviX as a vendor to his company and asked, *how do you know NoviX is our supplier?* Was his question framed to deflect the association? Ethan was about to respond with his own question, but Alyne beat him to the response. She said,

"We don't suspect; we know NoviX provides Solcom with solar panels. What we want to learn is, what are they used for?" Alyne stated bluntly.

"That, I'm afraid, is proprietary, my dear," Rick responded directly and followed up with a question. "How have you come by this information?" Rick directed his stare suspiciously at Jay.

The cat was out of the bag. Alyne wasn't careful. She hadn't spent years in an industry steeped in secrets, as had Ethan. She may not appreciate the nuances of discussing work of a classified nature, nor was she familiar with indirectly obtaining insight. She had tipped their hand, so Ethan offered more information to solicit answers.

"I've seen a solar panel from your payload. A panel supplied by NoviX." Ethan stated.

"You've seen one?" Rick inquired.

"I've seen one, yes. I'm aware that its design has a recovery feature. And I believe it's programmed to home into a specific location, a location in the Coral Sea. I have the coordinates," Ethan pointed to his comm-specs to indicate where he had the location saved.

"You have coordinates? That is most intriguing. I must say, now, you've piqued my interest in these fairings." Rick said.

"The Coral Sea?" Jay interrupted. "That's a remote area of the ocean, out far beyond the great barrier reef."

"How do you know about the Coral Sea?" Ethan

turned to Jay.

"The Coral sea is where our undersea cables from Brisbane join with the trunk line from Sydney and Guam. JAGS- Japan-Guam-Australia South (JGA-S)- the cable union is made a few hundred miles northeast of here."

Rick interrupted the Coral Sea discussion. "Why were you on your way to NoviX? What was your aim there?"

Alyne responded. "NoviX unique technology is export controlled. Export law prohibits them from selling the core technology to countries outside the commonwealth or sharing the technical know-how to manufacture the product. They can sell products that contain the technology, but not to just anyone. The Australian Government closely monitors international sales. Rocket Sci needs to ensure all of our suppliers comply with Export laws established by the Australian Department of Foreign Affairs and Trade. We are on our way there to find out what we can do to ensure Rocket Sci complies. At Rocket Sci, we don't have the Australian General Export Licences (AUSGELs) records that we suspect NoviX to have on file that enables them to supply to a Chinese company like Solcom."

"I see," said Rick. "And you expect they will tell you? They have signed a proprietary information agreement with Solcom. It's unlikely that they will offer that information to you." Rick paused and looked into Alyne's expectant face. He turned to Cross. "What if we go there together?"

"To NoviX? You think they'll be more likely to speak to us with you there?" Cross replied

"No. No. No. Not to NoviX, to the Coral Sea. Let's go to the location where you say the fairings are recovered. That's sure to shed some light on this mystery."

Cross realized the idea of going to the coordinates he had obtained hadn't crossed his mind. It hadn't come up in his discussions with Alyne either. Presumably, each of them had assumed that there was nothing there in the middle of the ocean to see. Why had they not considered such an obvious idea? Did she know something that he didn't? Alternatively, boating far out into open water required a vessel that neither Cross nor Alyne had the means to secure or charter. Going to the middle of the ocean to satisfy their curiosity, to search for floating hardware, or to await the next launch was such a wild idea that it didn't enter into the realm of actions they had at their disposal to consider until now.

"We can take the Intellagama. We can fly right over the spot and have a look. We can be back here in a few hours. In time for a late dinner," Rick pressed.

It was a compelling proposition; A chance to learn more about the mysterious fairings—a ride on the Intellagama.

"Sounds, MagiX." Alyne quipped, winking at Ethan, proud of her play on words using the Intellagama's manufacturer in her response. Magic indeed thought Ethan. If Rick wasn't involved, maybe. He smiled wearily.

The proposition evoked memories of the trio's excursion in Dubai. Was Cross being goaded to agree? Was his competitiveness clouding his judgment? What did she see in Rick?

"MagiX? NoviX? Should I start ending words in X? What the heX?" Jay was drunk. Kelsy glared. Chan responded.

"iX. It means 'of the ion' in Chinese. The Intellagama is MagiX's debut product, a result of corporate collaboration between Australia and China. NoviX solar panels operate at the ion level and are integral to the plane's design providing almost limitless power for daytime flight. I hope that Solcom products will soon enjoy similar success with the NoviX nanotechnology." Rick explained. "So what do you say, Mr. Cross? Are you up for the adventure? We'll do a flyby of the spot in question and head on back here."

Cross weighed his options. He stole a glance at Alyne, who seemed to have no hesitation. Was she an adventure junkie, or was there something more between her and Chan? Cross wondered if there would be an opportunity to best Rick in front of Alyne?

"I'm in, but on one condition." Cross paused for Rick to take the bait. He bit.

"What's that?"

"I buy the hot cocoas," Cross flashed his blue eyes at Alyne.

Alyne and Rick chuckled at the inside joke and the memory of Cross' offer for an après ski hot cocoa in Dubai. Hot chocolate would be no more out of place on a flight toward the equator in the middle of the Coral Sea than it would have been after skiing in the desert.

"It's decided then. Let's depart straight away. Maybe you can share other knowledge you have about the fairings, and perhaps I can answer some of your questions along the way." Rick suggested.

The whole proposition concluded quickly. Cross made arrangements for himself and Alyne to crash with Jay and Kelsy through Monday morning. As Cross paid the bill, Jay pulled him aside to say, "See you tonight. Be careful up there, Ethan. There's something I don't trust about this Rick head."

"Thanks. I'll have her back before dark. Keep the light on for us, dad." He razzed his friend's protective gesture but appreciated it nonetheless. Cross wasn't sure if he could fully trust anyone on the flight now, but his thirst for knowledge and answers won the day.

Before Cross knew it, they had parted ways with Jay and Kelsy and were boarding Rick's dinghy on the way to the Intellagama anchored just offshore in the river.

"How do you get this tinny into that plane?" Alyne asked Rick.

Smiling proudly, Rick keyed the handset of a radio built into the small boat to communicate with the assistant at the floating aircraft's controls. His command transmitted from the short antenna mounted on the bow ahead of the windscreen.

"Lower the rear gate. We're on our way back to the Dragon." Chan grinned at Alyne as the rear deck of the seaplane began to lower into the river water, "That's how." Chan switched channels and made a radio call to the Brisbane Airport Tower to announce their impending departure. Cross was jealous of Rick's fancy toys.

"Brisbane Departure, Solcom Dragon One off-site southwest of airfield on the river, requesting direct departure to the northeast, Brisbane Departure." Chan shifted the frequency back to the intercom channel to transmit to his pilot.

"I've called the Brisbane Tower for a direct departure; listen for their response on 133.45 MegaHertz."

"That's cool," said Cross. "The radio is an intercom and covers the Aviation band?"

"It covers more than that. It's a software-defined radio. Just input any frequency you desire. It covers marine and aviation bands. It's good for about 100 km. MagiX has thought of everything."

| Chapter 14 |

The Coral Sea
South Pacific

Through the wide rounded panes of the Intellagama's passenger windows, sunshine spilled in like gold. It had been nearly an hour and a half since they departed the Brisbane River. After having taxi-ed back to Victoria Bridge, engaging the twin electric jet engines, and lifting off the water's surface into a headwind gusting off the harbor, the explorers soared over the Goodwill river crossway. The aquatic aircraft was fueled by sunlight, and its occupants were propelled by intrigue.

The trio spent the first hour of the flight discussing what was known about the rocket fairing. Cross shared the timeline since Dubai and what he had learned. He explained that the US Army facility at Kwajalein had come to possess a fairing after recovering the component floating in the sea. He described how he was able to recognize portions of the code as guidance control laws, and that's where Cross had discovered the latitude and longitude coordinates that he had passed to Chan's assistant. This man was now piloting the electric jet into the heart of the Coral Sea.

Alyne picked up on the narrative where Cross had left off. She explained that she and Cross had traveled to

Rocket Sci headquarters to learn who supplied the solar panel component. They discovered that NoviX provided the nanotech solar panels and that Australia may regulate the technology by EAR and ITAR export control laws. Rocket Sci had no other records, so they arranged their appointment on Monday to speak directly with the supplier. After a few simple questions, Rick had excused himself from the passenger cabin to join his assistant in the cockpit.

They traveled in Intellagama high luxury at 650 mph above the ocean when Rick spoke from the pilot's cabin via the Intercom system. Upfront, Chan pretended to be the pilot as his silent assistant manned the controls.

"Please fasten your seatbelts; we are arriving at our destination. Please be cautious when removing your items from the overhead bins, as things may shift during touchdown."

"We're landing?" Cross sat up and looked at Alyne. "I thought we were just doing a flyover of the coordinates I provided?"

Alyne turned her palms up and raised her brow at Ethan. "Me too," she said as Rick emerged from the cabin.

"I know what you're thinking, we didn't discuss landing, but I didn't want to spoil the surprise. I've picked up a set of personal-sized scuba equipment. I've been dying to try them out. The reef will be an extraordinary opportunity to christen them and see some exotic sea life. The Great Barrier Reef is over 400 miles away, just 100 miles off the Australian shore; we are over 500 miles away from the nearest land. Just think we may see things that no one else has ever explored. I've got wet suits for each of you." He made his way to the rear of the passenger compartment to where a sealed door separated the occupant compartment from the unpressurized boat hold where the skiff was stowed. Rick opened a slim cabinet door and removed a duffle bag containing water bottles and scuba gear for the expedition. At the bottom of the locker, a black and orange sack was shoved out of sight. Chan quickly closed the door.

"Hold on," said Alyne, "Reef? Are we really doing scuba?"

"Scuba, yes." Rick extracted three tiny compressed air bottles from the bag.

"Aren't you supposed to wait 24 hours before flying after scuba diving?" Cross asked. Alyne concurred with a nod. Chan explained.

"We will stay close to the surface, under 20ft down, where there is no concern of decompression sickness. Besides, we can fly the Intellagama low back to Brisbane."

Cross asked his question next. "20ft? That's not very deep. What are we going to see out here in the middle of the ocean at that depth? The sea floor could be miles deep." *And diving?* He thought, *didn't he tell Chan that the fairings float?* He suppressed the stories Alyne had shared with him on Bondi; the rip tides, the sharks, and of course, the tiny, silent, and deadly Irukandji jellyfish. Out here, they didn't even have red flags for protection.

"Oh, it's not deep out here, not more than 60 feet, I'd say." Chan cited the figure. "Some places you could even Snuba dive if we had the right gear." Rick laughed at himself. Cross looked at Alyne but said nothing. *Had Rick been here before? What was Snuba diving?* "What do you say, Cross? You in?" Rick roughly shoved a folded red and blue wet suit into Cross's chest, pushing him off balance in the bobbing watercraft.

"I'm in," Cross responded, grinding his teeth.

"Me too." Alyne said with a smile as Rick gently handed her a wet suit, "What an adventure. This is gonna be a ripper!" Alyne stepped into the aircraft's tiny water closet to change with the tote bag containing the suit that Rick had politely handed to her.

The low afternoon sun peered from the western sky into the luxurious cabin through the aircraft's port side portals. Cross and Rick pulled on their wet suits. Chan turned his back to Ethan, gesturing for help to be zipped up. Cross turned and did the same. Rick handed Cross a dive knife to strap to his ankle. "Always dive with a knife. It could save your life." Rick said.

Alyne emerged from the lavatory. Four millimeters of Neoprene traced the curves of her body. The tight-fitting garment accentuated her feminine physique. It seemed as if she was poured into the flattering suit. It was the polar opposite of the unflattering square-cut parka she wore in Dubai on their first adventure.

"Can one of you Bruces zip up my cozzie? I don't want to look like a shark biscuit."

Both men fumbled to her aid.

Alyne tossed the duffle bag on the floor at Cross's feet. "Throw your clothes, thongs, and sunnies in here— no room in those buggy smugglers for your effects. You ready? This is defo going off." Cross obliged, stuffing his sport coat, shoes, and comm-specs into the duffle bag.

Rick opened the sealed hatch to the rear compartment of the jet. He stepped in and released a lever. The plane's rear hatch automatically lowered, revealing the open water beyond. The small boat dropped from its overhead location, suspended from its secure stowed charging position on the ceiling of the seaplane. The silent man with no hair remained in the pilot's chair behind the yoke at the aircraft's pointy end. Rick barked instructions to him.

"Hold the Water Dragon here. We are deplaning. Each of us has about 15 minutes of air, so we'll be back shortly."

Rick tossed two life jackets into the small vessel as he vaulted the carbon fiber skiff's side and beckoned for Cross and Alyne to join. Rick offered a hand to assist Alyne as she captivatingly stepped over the threshold, dropping the tote into the boat. Rick motored a few meters from the waiting plane, stopped the engine, and tossed an anchor attached to a polymer-covered steel braided cable overboard. Cross could see the reef below through the pristine crystal water. Rick passed out flippers, masks, and a water bottle-sized compressed air tank to each diver. A mouthpiece with a breathe-time indicator was affixed to each bottle's built-in regulator.

In no time, Rick had tipped himself backward over the edge of the boat into the water. Alyne followed next. Cross followed them into the blue. The trio bobbed on the surface together as Rick offered final instructions for the dive crew from behind his mask.

"Have a look around. Stay within a radius of the anchor line. If you need to surface before your timer is up, this is the sign." He mimed a cut-throat motion to his neck. "We'll meet back here at the boat." Rick bit the mouthpiece of his regulator, and he submerged. Alyne followed. Cross took a deep breath putting jellyfish and the other potential dangers of the sea to the back of his mind. Instead, he thought *maybe I'll spot some Paua shell to give to Alyne. That'll rival the silly dragon jade chocker necklace Rick had given Alyne earlier.*

As Rick had promised, the reef was majestic. It was teaming with life. Brightly colored fish abound. Small schools of tiny squid jetted their way across the coral in rhythm with the early evening sunlight that scintillated through the sky-clear water. Cross approached a parrotfish near the shallow ocean floor. He could hear the peck of its beak as it fed off the coral. Cross' attention moved from the fish to a ray passing nearby another 15 feet below him. It was blue in color. Cross recalled that blue light penetrated water more readily than other visible light wavelengths. The superior transmissibility of blue light in water was why objects, like the ray, appeared bluer. The path of the sea creature lifted his gaze upward.

Cross could see the wavy silhouette of the Intellagama a distance away and above his dive group. Rick had kicked his way nearer to the plane than Cross and Alyne. Above Cross was the small tender whose leaf-shaped hull bobbed like the floater of a fishing lure at the end of the plastic-sheathed anchor cable. Cross fixed his eyes on Alyne, who was slightly above him. She was busily swimming after another parrotfish, with pectoral fins that looked more like wings as it soared ahead of Alyne. She kicked her legs in unison, powerfully in pursuit. Her body moved like a dolphin. The sun framed her thin hourglass torso as she passed between its rays and Cross. She commanded as much attention as any exotic fish in the Coral Sea.

Soon, Rick gave the cutthroat signal to his companions from far through the water. Cross figured his exertion from kicking the 10, or 20-meter distance toward the plane had used up his air reserve at a faster rate than Cross or Alyne, who remained near the anchor line as instructed.

The few minutes of scuba diving around the beautiful remote coral reef, while memorable, yielded no clues. There was no paua shell and no sunken treasure at what seemed like the logical end of their quest. Rick surfaced at the rear gate of the Intellagama as Cross and Alyne rose by the boat. They each reached up to hold onto the edge of the low carbon hull. They watched Chan pull himself up onto the open gangplank of the airplane's lower rear hatch and stood. They awaited an explanation for his early ascent. Ocean water lapped the advanced aircraft as Chan pulled off his scuba mask and cleared his throat to shout to them.

"Mr. Cross. No sign of the solar panel fairings, I'm afraid. You should know that they are critical to Solcom's satellite infrastructure. NoviX's technology is the key enabler to our high-speed download service." Something felt off. Why was Chan talking tech from fifty feet away? "One day, perhaps NoviX technology will make it into Solcom satellites too. After all, modern communications satellites are power constrained. Even with huge banks of photovoltaic solar cells, my Icarus satellites have no more than 4000 or 5000-watt power envelopes. Using NoviX cells, the same weight of panels could result in a tenfold increase in power budget. Furthermore, since NoviX cells can convert infrared radiation, normally lost as heat, into power, the satellites will have less difficulty staying cool in direct sunlight."

"Why are you talking about this now, Chan? I thought you used up all your hot air?" Alyne smirked at Cross.

"I'm telling you because currently, Solcom doesn't use NoviX technology for this application. I'd like to one day, but unfortunately, I won't have that opportunity if you continue to pose the kind of export compliance questions you have been, Cross. I can't have you interfere with the acquisition meeting on Monday. Too many years, too many millions have gone into preparation for this moment." The mood was beginning to turn. "I simply can't have you poking around calling attention to Solcom's current dealings with NoviX. Nothing can come into question while I finalize the procurement of the company. Their technology is too important to the ecosystem of Solcom's communication infrastructure. Surely you can understand that?"

Alyne spoke next. "What are you saying, Rick? Would you have us go back to Sydney or New Zealand empty-handed? We've come a long way just to tie off directly with NoviX on the matter."

"Yes, I'm saying go home. Go home or wait until NoviX is mine. I'm happy to strike a new accord with Rocket Sci as soon as the paperwork transfers to my name. I can't imagine there will be an issue when we become an even larger customer to Rocket Sci." Cross felt Chan was plotting something nefarious.

"What are you telling us, Chan?" Cross asked. Rick's

monologue was feeling more and more like a sinister soliloquy.

"I'm saying I'll be back for you. Back for you both." Chan gazed at Alyne. "There is business at NoviX that needs my attention, and the sun is low on the horizon. The Intellagama doesn't fly in the dark."

"Don't do it, Chan!" Cross shouted as Chan swung himself into the belly of the dragon and commanded his assistant to close the rear hatch. The electric engines fired up, and the amphibian began to taxi away.

Alyne hurled some Australian cuss words.

"Rick, you slack-arse moll! You can stick that rocket launch contract up your arse, ya bloody wanker!" she yelled as she vaulted herself into the tender of the low side.

Cross threw his flippers into the hull and scrambled into the boat, vainly thinking he might hoist the anchor and close the gap between the boat and aircraft using the tiny electric trolling motor. The water dragon was their only means to reach land.

It was futile. The jog in the boat plane's hull generated the cavitation needed to break the sea's surface tension. The powerful jet lifted into the sky, departing southwest into the sunset forever after eve. They were marooned in open water. Alyne began to cry hysterically as the gravity of their peril set in. They were over 500 miles from the nearest land.

"He left us. He left us. I'm not a crier. I'm not a crier. I don't cry."

"Not crying will have to wait," Cross told Alyne as his mind worked to evaluate their fate. This was not a time for emotion. He finished pulling up the plastic-covered steel anchor line and hooked the weight to a holding cleat. "Turn on the radio." Cross pointed at the radio in the boat's basic dash panel. He stumbled across the small rocking hull. The last frequency entry was likely tuned to the Intellagama's cockpit. He clutched the radio's handset and shouted into it.

"Chan, this is Cross. Come get us. Come back here, Rick!"

It was no use. Even if Rick heard them, he would not return. He couldn't. The Intellagama had only enough time before sunset to make the trek back to Brisbane Harbor. Rick had timed it precisely. Leaving them was his plan from the start.

He tuned the dinghy's radio. It was a basic software-defined radio like those first developed for military applications. It had arrows to the left and right to adjust the frequency. It had a touchpad to enter any specific frequency from low AM radio around 535 kHz, through the familiar FM spectrum through 108 MHz, above that to 135 MHz at the top end of the aviation band, and into the VHF frequency range assigned by the FCC to marine services topping out at 174 MHz. It was a highly configurable radio, presumably, so it could talk to maritime vessels and aircraft. Cross knew a radio like this would have its transmit power regulated to be less than 25 watts. Its range would be no more than 60 miles, just as Rick had mentioned in the Brisbane River.

Cross didn't know any specific communications frequencies, let alone emergency channels. He racked his brain. The only radio frequency he could recall was the frequency that Doctor Dodge had mentioned. The frequency for the HAM station he wanted to reach; the station that had gone silent key. The one that shared the same year as the Sea Gull schooner that had vanished exploring the Pacific islands? 1836? Yes. 1836 kHz. Cross keyed in the number to tune the radio. 1.836 MegaHertz. He pressed the Citizen's Band-like handheld transmitter and spoke.

"Come in. Come in. Ethan Cross to Sea Gull." Cross tried to hail the old man via Shortwave HAM. No answer. The radio wasn't powerful enough. Kwajalein was too far away.

"What about the motor?" Alyne said. "At least we have that."

Cross looked at it. "We'll need to conserve it. It'll never get us five or six hundred miles."

"Well, how far will it get us?" Alyne asked eagerly.

"Well, let's guess the battery in this thing is a 100 amperage hour. A motor like that might draw, let's say, 25 amps. So that's 4 hours we could run at top speed before running out of energy." Cross fumbled around in the low light. "MagiX didn't bless this dinghy with any of their solar tech, so we have no way to charge it either."

"Can't we go slower to get back to land?" Alyne asked, despair in her voice.

"I'm guessing this thing goes about 5 miles per hour. In 4 hours, we could get about 20 miles. We might as well save the energy for the radio." Cross reasoned. Chan must have done the same math. Even if they could run the motor indefinitely, it would take four or five days to get back to Brisbane. Cross checked for oars, but there were none. Even his years of competitive rowing would be of no help for a 500-mile trek. Chan didn't have to worry about them interfering with his meeting on Monday, that was for sure.

"And the radio? How far can we reach with that?"

"Probably no more than 60 miles, but let's keep trying," Alyne threw her hands up, huffed, and sat back down on the floor of the boat.

The sun had set over the Coral Sea. The last few minutes of twilight passed quickly as darkness rushed in. Ethan and Alyne were alone on the dark side of the planet. Cross gazed at the horizon to the West, where the sun had set. He turned his gaze slightly south from there to the direction where the Intellagama had vanished. Something primal in the back of his mind secretly hoped through the darkness that maybe Chan would come back for them from that direction. Rationale, though from his frontal lobe, reasoned it to be unlikely. Besides, the Itellegama couldn't make the trip until sunrise now. They were stranded.

Cross tilted his head back and stared up at the night sky, now filled with stars. It resembled a backlit canopy with holes punched in it. With no light pollution from human settlements anywhere for hundreds of miles, the stars seemed brighter than he had ever seen. They were a strange, unfamiliar jumble of unrecognizable constellations to Cross like the photo of the glow worm caves Alyne had explained in New Zealand. There was no Big Dipper, no Orion's belt. He felt far-far from home. The other side of the planet was a lonely place. He noticed Alyne gazing up as well. Perhaps the sky didn't look so strange to her. The warm South Pacific air hugged his skin. He wanted to move closer to Alyne.

"Chan must have planned this from the start," Cross said to Alyne across the small boat. "No way for us to interfere with his plans for Solcom now. I guess we were right about him being involved with illegally exporting NoviX technology." Cross still wondered what exactly Chan was doing with the solar panels? Solving the mystery was feeling less critical now than surviving.

"Naw, Yeah," Alyne responded, her mind in a different place. "Would you rather be right, Ethan, or would you rather be safe?" She wasn't in the mood to discuss the case. Cross pondered her question. She was right. It wasn't the first time his relentless pursuit of facts got him into a bind. Cross stared into the darkness squinting to separate the horizon from the sky.

A strand of blue flickers caught the corner of his eye a couple of miles ahead due west. Cross turned his head to the right to stare straight in the direction of the flickers. He saw nothing. Again, he turned his head slowly back to the southwest. There, he saw the blue glimmers again in his peripheral vision. Cross knew that peripheral vision uses mostly rods and almost no cones. He was familiar with the human eye's photoreceptor physiology because of its parallel to Electro-Optic sensors. Eyes have two types of light-sensitive cells, called cones and rods. Our central vision uses an area densely packed with cones sensitive to color and needs ample light to function well. Peripheral vision uses mostly rods, which are sensitive to movement. He briefly recalled his fox bat encounter in Sydney when the creature's swift movement had drawn his attention. The rods in his eye could also quickly pick up changes in brightness and perform better at night.

He rubbed his eyes and looked again. Yes. Tiny flashes of blue shimmered in the distance. He could see them in the corner of his vision. The twinkles looked a bit like falling snow. He couldn't see it well, but he perceived they were occurring in a long column as high as he could view in the night sky.

"Alyne, do you see that?" He pointed west, "Am I

seeing things, or do you see specs of light beaming from the surface of the water over there on the horizon?"

Alyne sat up and turned her gaze to the west.

"No. I don't see anything, Ethan."

"Use the corner of your eye. Your peripheral vision is more sensitive."

There was a long pause from Alyne before she spoke, "Oh, yes. I see twinkles. Blue twinkles. That way." she pointed west.

"Pass me the duffle bag, please. I need my comm-specs."

"You're gonna dawn your sunnies at night?" Alyne posed a reasonable question.

Ethan switched on the glasses and looked due west. He checked for a phone signal. There was none. He saw nothing through the polarized lenses. Cross switched on the infrared vis feature using the ear stay button. Nothing. That feature was useless. He pulled up the image he had snapped of the coordinates.

20° 8' 29" S, 158° 37' 4"E (-20.14159, 158.61803)

Latitude 20 degrees, 8 minutes, 29 seconds South, Longitude 158 degrees, 37 minutes, 4 seconds East.

He checked the current location provided by the comm-specs. The low-power radio frequency signal from Global Positioning Satellite ephemeris transmissions could reach the device anywhere in the world. Despite knowing their precise location, the irony was that they had no way to communicate where they were. His comm-specs displayed:

Latitude 20 degrees, 8 minutes, 29 seconds South, Longitude 158 degrees, 39 minutes, East

"That bastard. Chan dropped us East of my coordinates!"

"What!? How far East?"

"2 minutes. Do you know how far 2 minutes is at this longitude?" He flipped on the quiet motor and steered the rudder West toward the blue lights.

"Actually, I do. One degree of longitude at the equator equals about 100 kilometers. So one minute at the equator is about just over a kilometer, or if you prefer, 1 minute at the equator is approximately one nautical mile. We are south of the equator- just above the tropic of Capricorn- so our minutes are shorter. I'd say we're less than two clicks away." Cross looked at Alyne, impressed with her deduction. "Occupational hazard of an orbital launch coordinator." The director of launch and mission integration smirked in the darkness.

"Those blue lights are just about as far away as we

can see then. The horizon is no more than three miles from our vantage point here in this tiny boat." Cross recalled another fact he had learned from Dr. Dodge.

It took nearly 30 minutes as the trolling motor strained to propel them through the ocean toward the mysterious blue stream of lights. As they neared the location, the sea's surface looked like a thousand diamonds strewn across a blue blanket. Cross quickly dismissed his hypothesis that the blue lights were some sort of bioluminescence. The light wasn't coming from the surface. It was coming from above and seemed to be emanating from some unseen origin traveling swiftly across the entire night sky, pointing steadily at Cross' coordinates as it passed. *A satellite*, he thought. Again, Cross put on his comm-specs. He peered into the shallow water below through the sparkling surface using his comm-specs' infrared night vision mode.

Cross could see heat signatures a few meters below them in the water. The glowing shapes looked like giant leaves of a large fern splayed out on the ocean floor. They emitted IR light which had a longer wavelength than the visible blue light that the shapes were absorbing. The leaf-like forms appeared to glow through his comm-specs' IR-vis feature just as the handle of his backpack had been visible when exposed to shorter wavelength UV light in the dark nightclub. The nanotech material was glowing in the near-infrared spectrum, re-emitting energy absorbed in the shorter blue light wavelengths. A dark line formed the spine of the strange symmetric underwater formation. It passed through the middle of the synthetic petals, which fanned out like thin leaves from either side of the stem. The array stretched on for thousands of feet, as far as he could see in either direction through the crystal water. It was like an unfurled Koru fern frond he had learned about from Beck Peters at Rocket Sci. It looked alive. It was beautiful. The mirrored row of electronic leaflets snaked away below them. The solar panels!

"Alyne, look into the water!" Cross handed her his comm-specs.

"The Rocket fairings! There they are on the ocean floor!" Alyne said.

Cross's mind raced. Chan had said his Icarus constellation beamed high volumes of information to the surface. Chan mentioned Solcom's satellites used lasercomm cross-links but failed to mention how they sent information down. Cross had wondered if Solcom's downlink also used lasers. Now he was sure. The blue light they had seen was from off-axis laser beams. All this time, Cross had assumed that by surface, Chan had meant the ground. Until now, Cross hadn't considered the ocean floor as part of "the ground." The pieces were falling into place. Solcom used the rocket fairings laced with the nanotech solar panels as a laser light receiver for Solcom's LEO satellite internet service downlink. Chan had said NoviX panels were the key to his high download speeds; now Cross understood why.

Cross took the comm-specs back from Alyne. He

could perceive a thin black line running between the panels. It formed the spine of the massive fishbone-looking arrangement. The panel leaflets were positioned to stem into the root of an undersea cable. The undersea internet cabling section ran right through the heart of the receiver panel array. Jay Blah had mentioned an undersea cable junction out here in the Coral Sea. Cross and Alyne had found it.

Of course! Cross remembered that NoviX solar cells had billions of little antennae, each roughly ¼ the wavelength of sunlight. Blue light was square in the middle of Ultraviolet and Infrared, and blue traveled best through the water. At night, Solcom was using the same panels that could make energy during daylight as a data downlink receiver in the dark of the sun.

Antennae! Cross had an idea. He fumbled for the life jackets. He grasped two.

"Go figure. Chan left us each a life preserver, but none for himself." Cross busied himself, tying them together. He reached over the side of their carbon fiber hulled craft and pulled the tiny anchor weight free from its hold. He tied the life-saving devices securely to the anchor cable and tossed the arrangement overboard.

"What are you doing?" Alyne said, extending her arm instinctively toward the floating safety gear carrying their anchor away from them over the surface of the water.

"Trust me," Cross said, kneeling to payout the anchor line with deliberate, measured arm lengths. He counted to himself as he provided instructions to Alyne.

"Can you pull up the calculator in my comm-specs?" Alyne obliged. "The Frequency is 1.836 MegaHertz. Enter this figure, please: 1,836,000, and hit the reciprocal key. That's the period. Do you remember the speed of light in meters per second?"

Alyne responded immediately with another figure she knew well from a carrier working with satellite communications, "300 million meters per second."

"Multiply by that figure. Then divide that by four." Cross pulled the dive knife from its sheath strapped to his shin.

"What are you up to, Cross?"

"What's the figure?" Cross said impatiently.

"40 meters, why?" Cross did some mental math. That's about 130 feet. He had reached a count of nearly that hand over hand as he paid out the floating anchor line.

"Switch on the comm-spec flashlight, please" Cross held the dive knife and waited for her to illuminate his hands. Soon the light came on. Cross scribed the plastic sheathing of the anchor line around the circumference of the cable. He moved five inches down the line and repeated the operation. Next, he sliced the cable longitudinally as if splaying a fish. Carefully he peeled away the insulation.

"Now, shine the light on the bow of the boat ahead of the windscreen above the radio. Look for the radio's antenna mast." He instructed Alyne as he carried the portion of the exposed steel cable in both hands to the nose of the tiny ship. Alyne's light cast on the radio's short antenna mounted on the windscreen. Cross touched the cable's exposed metal to the antenna and wrapped the splayed, exposed metal segment around it with several tight twists.

"I'm making the antenna longer. It's too short for shortwave radio signals. It needs to be at least a quarter of the wavelength of the frequency you want to pick up. You just helped me calculate the wavelength of a frequency a friend of mine checks every night." Cross waited.

A few minutes passed. Then they heard a voice.

"QC, Sea Gull here, QC, QC, QC. Come in VP6PAC" It was coming through the radio. Cross had left it tuned to the last frequency he had tried. 1.836 MHz.

Cross scurried to grasp the radio handset and quickly keyed it to respond.

"Doctor Dodge? It's Ethan Cross."

"Cross? Ethan Cross? What are you doing on this frequency? Are you on Pitcairn?"

"You'll never believe this, but I'm at those coordinates where the Rocket Fairings are guided. We need you to pick us up. Are you in the schooner?"

"Yes. Yes. I've got your position in the Coral Sea," Cross thought of all the sophisticated tech Doctor Dodge had at his disposal aboard the Ghost. He would spot them floating on the sea when he got closer with the forward-looking Infrared imaging camera. The direction-finding array atop the stealth boat would use interferometry to compare Cross' radio signal to a database of known phase differences from all directions. It would correlate a matching angle of arrival and compute a line of bearing on which Dodge would point the Ghost to find them.

"I found your sticky note on my screen."

Or there was that, thought Cross.

"That location is almost a thousand miles from me," Dodge continued to transmit, "and from everywhere else, I might add! It'll take me about ten hours, but the Ghost is on its way. Keep the radio on this channel and transmit periodically. It'll help me get a final fix on you with the direction-finding array. I'll be able to resolve your bearing as I get closer. And Cross," There was a pause in the transmission as the old man chose his words. "How'd you know to reach me on this frequency?"

Cross keyed the radio, "1836, I remembered the date of that old schooner south Pacific exploration expedition you mentioned."

"The Sea Gull! I'm glad I told you the story!" The old man started to laugh as he released the transmission key.

Relieved, Cross enticed his rescuer with another carrot of info. "That's great! And you're never going to believe what we found out here."

Alyne was ecstatic. Relief was in her voice. "That was some clever thinking, Sherlock." She hugged Ethan, rocking the boat. They knelt together to stabilize the craft. She hugged him tighter.

"I thought you were into Chan?"

"Rick? Naw, he's a real Dick," Alyne whispered in his ear. Cross smiled in the dark.

Alyne tilted her head with her chin down and her eyes up. She smiled at Cross as she reached out in the darkness to touch his face.

| Chapter 15 |

The Ghost

It was early afternoon when the castaways got their first glimpse of the Ghost. Doctor David Archie Dodge was at the helm of his speedy stealth schooner. Cross and Alyne were tired and thirsty. They had been floating in their tiny boat in the middle of the Coral Sea for over ten hours since Rick Chan had departed in the Water Dragon, leaving them stranded. They had shared the water bottles at the bottom of the duffle bag, but those were gone now, and they were thirsty. They were tired and famished.

Their rescuer cued the radio from his approaching Schooner, "You're a sorry-looking crew. I've got you on the FLIR. I'm about 3 miles out." Doctor Dodge transmitted.

"Good to hear your voice!" Cross responded ecstatically through the radio's hand set.

Alyne raised her arms in triumph. She asked Cross, "I hope his sailboat has a loo. I need more than a pommie shower!"

In less than 5 minutes, the eerie-looking stealth ship was just off the tiny boat's starboard side, settling low on its supercavitation pylons as Dodge slowed the craft to rescue the stranded duo. A boarding gate lowered to the water between the dual stanchions from under the swath's belly. Cross motored the dinghy toward the larger vessel. A voice emerged first before a body.

"Cross, how'd you get way out here in that rowboat?" Doctor Dodge hobbled to the loading ramp.

"Are we glad to see you! Long story." Cross said, introducing his companion, "This is Alyne Jimmie with Rocket Sci." He tossed a length of the anchor line onto the deck for Archie to recover. The Doctor pulled them in.

"Ahoy, Mate." Alyne shouted, "Thank you! I like your sailboat." Alyne said to the Doctor as she glared at Cross, "Schooner?" she inquired with manufactured annoyance.

Cross smiled as he shared a moment with Archie. He started his exchange with Doctor Dodge as Alyne climbed onto the Ghost ship's lowered gangplank.

"You'll never guess what we found out here," Cross stated.

"Start talking. I've been waiting ten hours for this story." Doctor Dodge was a direct man. "There are towels, water, and food in the gally. Help yourself to the head." He directed his offer to Alyne as she climbed up the ramp. She made her way directly to the lavatory. Cross climbed abord the Ghost's lowered hatch, grabbing the tote bag and leaving Rick's dinghy adrift in the Coral Sea.

"Solcom appears to be using the panels as lasercomm receivers for their downlink from their Icarus satellites. They are installed on the ocean floor. It's not deep out here." Cross offered the first missing puzzle piece.

"Lasers from space? Through the water?" Doctor Dodge asked.

"Yes. Blue Lasers penetrate the water. The downlink starts at night. All the fairings are positioned along an undersea cable. I've no idea how they are installing them down there."

"That's incredible. The sea acts as a giant filter for other frequencies and allows only blue light wavelength to reach the receiver? Intriguing. How deep is the array?"

"No more than 30 feet deep where it's installed along the cable, I'd guess."

"That install work could be accomplished via Snuba equipment from a surface ship pretty readily. We use Snuba all the time for equipment maintenance in the lagoon at Kwaj."

"Snuba? What's that?" asked Cross. Chan had used the term.

"It's when your air tanks are floated on the surface, and the diver breathes via a hose. If someone on the surface is managing the supply, a diver can stay down much longer." Cross remembered Chan's off-handed

Snuba reference and scowled inwardly.

"Where do you want me to take you?" Dodge asked Cross.

Alyne responded as she emerged from the head, wiping water from her hair and face with a towel. She looked refreshed from a quick rinse.

"Can you take us back to Brisbane? How long with that take?" Alyne was livid at Chan. She wasn't about to let him get away without a fight. Cross could see she was working out how to enact her revenge.

"It's five hundred miles or so to Brisbane from here. It'll probably take 6 or 7 hours. You're lucky I was fueled for a long trip! I can top off in port there and pick up supplies. It'll be a welcome detour."

"That'll work. We may still make it in time to get to NoviX on Monday." Alyne figured out loud.

"You got a phone aboard?" Cross asked Dodge and then looked at Alyne. "I can have Jay meet us at the port and take us there in his Cadillac."

"Yes. A Caddy? Sounds fancy. I haven't seen a real car in years." Doctor Dodge commented.

"It's older than your Jeep-kart. It may even be older than the Ghost!" Cross replied. "It's got an old gas motor."

"Those are solid cars. Heavy. Rare find in Australia, I suspect. They don't make them like that anymore." The old man reflected.

"Where were you headed when we radio-ed you?" Cross asked as he found a seat on a comfortable cot that folded down from the wall.

"I was on my way to vacation in Tahiti when your signal came through. I am off to watch the solar eclipse. It's one of the only natural events that reduces the natural background radio noise from the sun. Good for HAM-ing. I'll try Pitcairn again for a few minutes as the shadow passes over the island. MSIC headquarters finally approved my request to travel there via the Ghost. It seems the ship is a Ghost to them now." The older man chuckled at his own joke. "They care less these days about protecting its aged-out tech. I can make a pitstop in Brisbane. You're just lucky I was fueled up for a trip of that distance." The Doctor explained the fortune of their encounter on the high seas. Alyne spoke up again.

"Why did you ask us if we were on Pitcairn? Is that a place?" Alyne asked the Doctor about the odd reference upon first radio contact with them. Cross remembered the man's obsession with contacting every South Pacific island via HAM. He waited for Dr. Dodge to explain how Pitcairn had gone Silent Key.

"Pitcairn was the last holding of the British Empire in the Pacific." The Doctor cleared his throat, readying himself for his story, as he engaged the Ghost's powerful torpedo-like engines. The swath rose on its stanchions. Dodge pointed the vessel southwest toward Brisbane as he began his tale, "It's a place, so remote, so unlikely, and so lost in time that it seems more myth than reality. But the place is real, all right. The island rises alone out of the South Pacific, more than 3,000 miles from any continent. Its nearest neighbor is the equally enigmatic Easter Island of more fame. Pitcairn is a hunk of red volcanic rock not much larger than the Boston Common. The relentless open sea has pounded at it for millennia, creating a fortress of 500-foot cliffs. The mystery of Pitcairn has become even more alluring to me since I learned it had gone silent key."

"Silent Key?" Alyne prompted the storyteller.

"Silent key is a phrase we use when a station goes inactive. Sadly, it's usually when a fellow HAM operator passes away."

"People live on Pitcairn?" Asked Cross.

"For many years, yes. There is just enough vegetation, coconut, and breadfruit to support a small population. It has lured dreamers and adventurers for three centuries. Its history has been rife with scandal and intrigue since even before Fletcher Christian, and his tiny band of rogues with their Tahitian wives happened upon it. They famously found it during their escape from the British Navy in 1789. They made the elusive island their hideout. They burned and sank their own ship, stranding themselves to stay hidden. They seemed to disappear from the face of the earth. They vanished from those seeking to avenge one of the greatest maritime heists of all time, the mutiny on the Bounty."

"That's fascinating. Are you retracing Fletcher's steps, Dodge? Planning to take a Tahitian wife to Pitcairn? Now I want to know more." Cross leaned in.

"You wouldn't be the first. The tale has captured the world's imagination for centuries, inspiring a novel by Jules Verne, a story by Mark Twain, scores of other books, and one blockbuster movie after another—five in all. The first was an Australian silent film. Later, Fletcher Christian became Errol Flynn, then Clark Gable, Marlon Brando, and Mel Gibson. I've seen them all. A dashing new hero for each generation."

"Well, if it's so well known, it doesn't sound so remote or hard to find." Alyne offered.

"Oh, I assure you it is. Even the British couldn't find it again after rediscovering it in 1767 on a voyage led by Captain Philip Carteret. Carteret, who sailed without the newly-invented marine chronometer, had charted the island at 25°02′S 133°21′W longitude, and although the latitude was reasonably accurate, his recorded longitude was incorrect by about 3°. That's about 200 miles west of where the island is" Cross stole a glance at Alyne, reminded of how Chan had dropped them miles from their undersea quarry. "Even Robert Pitcairn, the crew member who first spotted the island, was lost at sea years later before ever finding it again. It's a place that doesn't want to be found."

"Are there people living there now?" Cross asked the storyteller.

"Well, that's the question. Twenty-five years ago, the population of the island was 56. It was clear sometime around 2020 that if nothing were done, only three working-age people would be left on the island by this time, with the rest being very old. Residents who had left the island showed little interest in coming back, and few expressed a desire to return. The Pitcairn government's attempts to attract migrants have been unsuccessful. As a British Overseas Territory, the British government was pressured to decide the island's future. I understand they sold the whole island to a corporation who relocated the remaining people about the same time that the island went silent key." Cross thought of how the US military had relocated the indigenous Marshallese from the Bikini Islands to Ebey near Kwajalein before testing atomic and hydrogen bombs there. A fact Dodge had taught him not long ago.

"Ok," Alyne conceded, "That is mysterious. A corporation? Do you know what interest a business would have in a remote island like that?"

"I'm afraid not. It could be anything. It's no more mysterious than Solcom guiding clandestine solar panels to the middle of the ocean. After all, you're here on the Ghost because a corporation is obtaining laser communication receivers illegally and installing them underwater to feed internet from satellites to undersea cables." The Doctor recounted their sensational findings.

"I suppose you're right about that." Cross stated, "It seems a corporation will go to great lengths to hide their subterfuge if there is sufficient profit to be had." Cross looked at Alyne, referring to Chan's illegal export of NoviX solar panel technology to Solcom and stranding them in the Coral Sea to keep it secret. "Still, designing a product that can be covertly delivered on a rocket and submerged in the sea seems like an overly complex effort simply to avoid export law. I wonder if there is something more sinister afoot with Chan's plans."

Alyne suggested to her detective partner, "Perhaps we'll make it to NoviX in time to crack this case and stop Chan from getting away with his crimes."

| Chapter 16 |

NoviX

Brisbane, Australia

"Has the acquisition meeting wrapped up?" Alyne asked the receptionist abruptly.

"Naw, Yeah, It's over," the polite Aussie administrative assistant replied. "They all but wrapped up an hour ago in there, save for what's left with the legal bits, and what have you. The winning party is in there finalizing the provisos." She craned her neck around to indicate that the meeting was occurring behind a closed mahogany door, her back at the other end of a short foyer. "Lot's of that paperwork with a foreign buyer, I imagine, but the deal is said and done. Is there someone you're here to see?"

"Rick Chan. Chief Technical Officer of Solcom." Cross fought the urge to add disdain to his tone of voice.

"Ah, the gentlemen from Solcom left earlier after the deal was concluded. Downtrodden fellows, I might say. Long trip home to China empty-handed, I imagine." She swiveled on her seat to reach for a garment. "They left in a hurry. One of the poor blokes forgot his sport coat, I'm afraid."

Cross was puzzled by the comment. He looked at Alyne. She wrinkled her brow and turned out her palms to Cross to signal her confusion.

"Solcom did not purchase NoviX?" Alyne asked

"No. Solcom was outbid. And handsomely, I understand. And from what I hear, the NoviX board members weren't keen on the direction they proposed to take the company's technology. The new buyers have pledged to focus on renewable energy applications in keeping with the NoviX vision. Isn't that grand? It's dardy for us here at NoviX. Is there anyone else I can hail for you?"

Alyne spoke slowly, "Yes, perhaps Mr. Roger Morrison in supply chain management. Tell him Alyne Jimmie of Rocket Sci is here to speak with him."

Alyne's face was filled with an unspoken question as she faced Cross to formulate a plan of action. Cross had another question for the receptionist.

"If Solcom lost the bid, who then has purchased NoviX?" Cross asked.

"An English outfit. I believe they are called...." The woman struggled to recall the acronym. "Energy

Ventures and Electronics Enterprises...or some such thing." It wasn't immediately familiar to Cross. "Have a seat here if you like, or you may find the collaboration center chairs a bit more comfortable." The receptionist pointed across the foyer to her left. To Cross's and Alyne's right, at a small open concept conference room with a pair of full floor to ceiling glass French-style double doors that faced the lobby. There was a long table lined with plush leather chairs beyond the pair of doors. There were glass boards and white walls designed for sharing concepts and sketches along the wall. Past the table, another large window faced the outdoors. They could see through the building and over an access road that ran along the structure and down the river bank. It was a pleasant view. It seemed like a welcoming area. The collaboration room was a bit more private than the lobby for Cross and Alyne to converse. Although Cross thought, the open concept did nothing to block the view of anyone entering the front door on their way to the main conference room. The gracious woman continued. "Help yourself to some water and biscuits. The tea should still be hot as well."

The pair of explorers thanked the receptionist and approached the small water cooler. Cross said to Alyne, "I should call Jay before he's too far off." Alyne nodded in agreement.

He lowered his comm-specs and pressed the ear stay button to recall the most recent contact. Cross recorded a voice-to-text message. "Jay, a dead-end at NoviX. We need a Fulton recovery. Thanks, man."

Cross poured some water into a small disposable cone cup and handed it to Alyne. He poured himself a cone as a man stepped out from the main conference room at the far end of the lobby, gently closing the mahogany door behind him as he answered a call, putting the comm-band on his wrist up to his ear. They could hear his side of the conversation as they each sipped their water.

"Alan Fortinbras, here, how may I help you?" he started.

"Ah, yes, Madame, It went well. NoviX is ours now. Laertes is in there with your father wrapping up the transaction presently."

There was silence for a moment.

"Yes, I'm sure we'll still be in session when you arrive then, Madame. Come right in. The conference hall is at the rear of the lobby, directly opposite the front door. Pass the reception booth. It's the wooden door directly across the foyer."

Cross looked at Alyne and shrugged. No clues in that conversation. Fortinbras wrapped up his call.

"Indeed, it'll be a nice façade for our efforts on Pitcairn. And who knows, we may even find utility for the panels there as well. It was a clever idea, Madame. Well done. See you, momentarily." Fortinbras ended the call and slipped back through the heavy mahogany door.

Alyne shrugged back at Cross. Pitcairn? That was a curious coincidence, thought Cross. They tossed their disposable water cups into the wastebasket. Cross nodded toward the collaboration room the receptionist had offered to them and proceeded. Alyne fell into step behind him. Here they would wait for this Morrison character, and more importantly, discuss their next move.

Cross reached for the French doors' lever-style handles with one hand on each grip. Lightly, he pushed forward to part the barrier like saloon doors but found they wouldn't yield. He turned the handles downward. Only the left hand swiveled. It was a minor fumble. It was clear the doors were meant to be pulled. The right-hand door was secured to the floor, and the ceiling with header and footer cleats locked into place. Cross took a step back to pull the free door toward them with his left hand as he swept his right hand across his body with a gentlemanly, "After you, Madame." He mocked Fortinbras' formal moniker.

"Thank you, Monsieur. You have to be 10% smarter than the object you're working with." Alyne razzed Cross as she passed. Cross smiled, and his heart skipped. She was adorable. They sat opposite each other at the table with large glass walls bookending the freshly occupied think tank. The Brisbane River lazily slinked by beyond the window while the lobby sat idle beyond the glass doors. The sterile white walls and switched-off glass boards lining the adjacent clean sketch panels were a visual parallel to the clean slate of ideas the collaboration room occupants faced.

"What now?" Alyne spoke first, "It sounds like Rick left empty-handed."

"People in glass houses shouldn't throw stones." Cross motioned to their glass surroundings. It seemed they, too, had come up empty. No more leads to follow. No one was left to question.

"Well, I feel like throwing a rock. I was looking forward to confronting Rick. Do you think he would have really come back for us?" Alyne was cute even when she was angry.

"I'm glad we didn't wait to find out." Cross finished his sentence as the lobby door opened. A woman in a clean white sleeveless one-piece business dress with a high collar tight around her neck entered. Her hair was obsidian black and glistened as she strode past the receptionist without acknowledging the greeting. Cross stopped breathing. On the woman's wrist, a wide silver bracelet with a green hiddenite gem swung by her hip. Her focus was that of a laser, and she was aimed at the mahogany door. She didn't look left at the receptionist. She didn't look right at the collaboration room. Cross's head turned and followed her across the barren tundra of the short lobby. He watched as she vanished behind the mahogany door.

"Mr. Cross? Ethan? Are you ok?" Alyne waved a hand at him to break his stare. "I know she's a looker, but have some manners." She said jokingly. "You know, I think that was the woman I spilled your ice coffee on in Sydney...." Alyne wrinkled her brow at the memory. "Ethan?" Cross looked like he had seen an apparition. The sight of Sirena caused him to stand so quickly that his sunglasses dropped from his forehead onto the bridge of his nose.

"Good," he said to Alyne. "She deserved that coffee stain. Do you remember that story I told you about London? About the woman who double-crossed me? And the man who was Moriarty?"

"Adler? The Woman?" Alyne asked with alarm in her voice.

"That's her! We must get out of here immediately." Cross stood fast. Through the tinted glass of his comm-specs, beyond the clear doors of the collaboration room, he saw the mahogany conference room door open again. The outline of a man's frame darkened the doorway. The swing of the conference room door faced the collaboration room. By the chance of the architecture's geometry and the sheer coincidence of a moment frozen in time, Cross' gaze locked with the man standing at the threshold. The man's sinister smile turned off as he found a new purpose in his exit. Nathan Cain bore down on Cross, the glass doors nearly opening with his stare. His stride pushed off the lobby floor like the piston of a locomotive steam engine beginning the first rotation of its drive wheels. The CEO of EV3 towed Alan Fortinbras, his CTO, down the rails toward the collaboration room. Cain pulled open the glass door wide before there was any chance for Cross and Alyne to untie from the tracks.

"Ethan Cross!" Cain's voice boomed as the engine hissed to a stop. "Haven't you turned up like a bad shilling? And to think, we're all here, on the other side of the world, because of you."

The man's presence filled the room, forcing Cross and Alyne to the far side. Cain stood at the head of the table, the French doors at this back. He gripped both sides of the narrow table as if he were about to flip it end over end.

"NoviX is EV3's now. The solar panel technology we have acquired is advanced enough for people to believe that it is the power source for any ARCELOR application we pursue. NoviX's nanoscale rectifying antennas are better than the photovoltaic technology they replace, but being better has its place, Mr. Cross. Newer, more advanced technologies will naturally replace older, less useful ideas. One day the world will be ready for the ARCELOR to revolutionize our way of life, sourcing power for everything we do. But that revolution must be paced. It must be deliberate. It must be controlled."

Cross seethed but said nothing. Again, he was trapped in a room with Cain being forced to be fed his maniacal rhetoric.

"You see, your awareness of the ARCELOR caused me to reassess. I asked myself, what attention would EV3 receive if you were to tell the world that EV3 possessed a small fusion reactor? What a disruption that would be to our goal. I thought I might discredit you, smear your reputation, and cast you as a Bob Lazar."

"What if I were to publish your secret anonymously?" Cross countered. It was more his style. Ethan dreaded the limelight that would surely come from leaking the news of a viable fusion reactor. He was familiar with the fate that befell Bob Lazar, whom Cain had referenced. The man had gone to the media with Top Secret information obtained from his employment at Area 51. Bob, afraid by threats to his life due to the information he possessed about alleged UFO technology, told the world what he had seen as a means to protect himself from an "accident" perpetrated by those who might stand to benefit if he were to disappear. Bob's formidable technical reputation was tarnished after coming out with what sounded like sensational fiction. He became the poster child of government cover-ups and has been an icon to conspiracy theorists ever since. It was not a fate that Cross welcomed.

"True," Cain responded. "I considered that you could reveal the ARCELOR anonymously—no good countermeasure to that. Not until the Intellagama flew around the world with NoviX technology, that is. That revolutionary feat gave me an idea. NoviX solar panel technology offers a veil under which we can operate in the open while we finalize our work to realize the full promise of fusion."

"So buying Novix is just a front? Their solar cell technology will be just a façade for ARCELOR applications? Or are you trying to sure up your place in revisionist history as the man who perfected both solar cell technology and portable fusion energy production?" Cross was following Cain's plan. Cain felt compelled to elaborate.

"You know Mr. Cross; it was only in retrospect that history views the Wright brothers' Flyer as the essential breakthrough in manned flight? Others flew before that. Hot-air balloons had already achieved flight, of a kind; gliders were around, too, though they couldn't take off or land without a catapult or a leap. One of the Wright brothers' first manned flights lasted fifty-seven seconds —was that flight? Maybe, maybe not. But no one can argue that their Kitty-hawk moment changed history."

"History favors the victor, true. We remember Linberg as the man who flew across the Atlantic first. No one remembers that Igor Sikorsky would have earned that credit if the Spirit of St. Louis hadn't beat him to it." Cross antagonized Cain as his mind raced to conjure an escape.

"Sikorsky? A brilliant man. What I find more impressive is Sikorsky's achievement 37 years later when an engine of sufficient power came into being. The VS-300 was the first successful helicopter. It used a single main rotor and a vertical-plane tail rotor configuration for antitorque. With floats attached, it became the first practical amphibious vertical take-off and landing aircraft, making nearly every place in the world accessible. Accessibility, Cross, accessibility made possible by a new power source. That's what makes Sikorsky's invention so much more remarkable. The helicopter was revolutionary because a power source with a sufficient power-to-weight ratio allowed him to realize his vision. It's like how MagiX combines Intellagama's electric jet engine and NoviX's solar panels to create something revolutionary. Revolutionary and accessible like the ARCELOR." Cain paused to glace at his comm-band. Cross was impressed by Cain's knowledge of the historical details about Sikorsky that few knew. He shook the thought that perhaps Cain wasn't the mad-man Cross believed he was.

"These are moments in time that we take for granted." Cain continued, "They changed the course of human history. So too, will the ARCELOR. It will be replicated when its secret becomes known, and the world will change overnight. The ARCELOR will provide a blueprint for infinitely sustainable energy. That is why we must time it right. NoviX's tech will allow us to delay that moment in time. Another feint- a calculated misdirection necessary, allowing us to finalize the true magic that fusion will offer humanity."

"Why? Why wait? The world is ready now. Were they not ready for the news 30 years ago at the 2012 London Olympics? Was the ArcelorMittal tower to be dedicated to the achievement?"

"Ahhh. Yes, you know your untold history. It was to be a retrospective Kitty-hawk moment that never happened. I'm afraid the world is still too young to handle the reality of clean, abundant energy. The ARCELOR will put the awe-inspiring power and beauty of a real star into the hands of humankind. Are we ready? Lest we forget what history teaches us? J. Robert Oppenheimer dedicated his early professional life to creating a weapon from Uranium's tendency to fission, that is, to split apart while releasing neutrons and an immense amount of energy in a runaway situation we now call the atomic bomb. From this technology, men of sound mind birthed the nuclear reactor, a true benefit to society, but only after the infamous invention was used against Japan in World War II and again in detonations destroying the pristine Pacific islands of Bikini Atoll. Later in his career, Oppenheimer vehemently opposed the newer, more lethal evolution of his concepts that led to the hydrogen bomb. A nuclear fusion-powered weapon triggered by his fission bomb. Men of dark heart, you see, took the same technology too far.

For what, Mr. Cross, might dark hearts plot to use the ARCELOR before the world is mature enough? I cannot allow that, Mr. Cross." Cain's soliloquy sounded like Mein Kampf, delivered by the author himself.

"I'm sorry that my knowledge of the ARCELOR spoils your little cruise line empire." Cross poured salt in the wound, revealing to Cain that he was wise to the fact that Cain operated a cruise line with ships fueled by

ARCELOR reactors.

Cain let out a murderous laugh. "Is that what you think this is about? Panacea?" Cain laughed again with Fortinbras. "How feeble is your vision. Do you really think that EV3 has been maturing ARCELOR technology for thirty years to operate a cruise line?" He laughed again with Fortinbras.

"Let me tell you, Cross, that as science advances, specific technologies evolve and improve. From time to time, technologies mature together, allowing Kitty-hawk moments. Inventors like Sikorsky see new ways to solve problems—industries reform around new approaches. Consider how the Internet, cell phones, comm-bands, and comm-specs have transformed our lives? Take NoviX's revolutionary carbon nanotube solar panels, for instance – the technology allowed MagiX to create the Intellagama. Look at how each of these examples has enabled new, more useful applications in areas not previously considered.

That is the promise of the ARCELOR, in due time. Attributing incremental advances to NoviX's carbon nanotube solar panels will bide that time. NoviX technology may offer EV3 another genuine product along the way. A drone like the CENTURI could be adapted to be a high altitude, solar-powered, continuously looping aircraft at the top of the atmosphere. An offering like that could replace Solcom's satellites, for instance. EV3 could offer more flexible, more easily upgradable internet service at a tiny fraction of the cost, should we choose to enter that market. Whatever the application, the world will believe the tenfold power to weight advantage offered by NoviX panels over photovoltaic cells. NoviX will shield EV3 from prying eyes and allow us to further ARCELOR technology deployment to our ultimate cause. NoviX solar cells can cast a shadow on our sun. You are rowboat at sea in a hurricane, Mr. Cross, and it's time we eliminate you as a variable. We cannot have you running about like a wild card that EV3 does not control."

Cain turned to Fortinbras and barked an order.

"Watch them while I collect Rosenstern." Cain's glare moved back to Cross as Cain strode for the exit.

"We cannot afford another man-hunt fiasco like the one you caused in London." Cain's intense stare shifted back to his CTO.

Fortinbras nodded at this master. Cain spun and steamed out through the operational French door on a vector to the lobby entrance. He exited the building on a mission to return with his security chief. Rosenstern. Cross feared the prospect of another encounter with Dante Rosenstern, Cain's loyal guard dog. He hoped the mountain of a man wasn't someone to hold a grudge for nearly being asphyxiated.

The tall, lanky Fortinbras approached Ethan and Alyne. "You're mine now," he said as he closed the distance to the captives. Slowly, two paces from them, he reached his right hand into the inside left pocket of his sharp blue suit coat and...

"Phhhhwack!" A force slammed against the side of his face. Fortinbras's head whipped away from the impact, and the lights went out of his eyes as his body fell unconscious to the floor. Alyne dropped her leg to the ground, finishing her roundhouse kick. She stood at the ready like a boxing kangaroo. A note pad and a pen slid from Fortinbras' limp grasp across the collaboration room floor as his body came to rest in a heap.

"You kicked him in the face!?" Ethan said to Alyne, astonished by the sudden maneuver.

"I thought he had a gun."

"A gun? What do you think this is an action movie? People don't go to corporate meetings with guns in their breast pockets. It was a notepad, look." Cross pointed at the splayed pad of paper on the floor. "Did you think he was going to kill us with questions?"

"Sorry, mate, your story about the chase in London and all that talk about eliminating you as a variable...."

"Nevermind that. Let's get out of here." They stepped over Fortinbras' unconscious body.

The pair hurried out of the collaboration center and toward the building's front door to exit. A few steps into their escape, they saw the receptionist stand and reach over her desk, holding a suit coat out to an Asian man coming through the NoviX main entrance to retrieve it. Rick Chan saw them as he entered the small lobby. He ignored the garment and advanced toward Alyne and Cross. On instinct, they retreated away from the threat in the only direction available to them, back into the collaboration room.

Rick shouted, "You!" pointing at them as he advanced.

Ethan's mind raced. They were back in the glasshouse. He spoke to Alyne as he reached to pull the glass door closed. "Quick, do you still have that necklace from Rick?"

Alyne thrust her hand into her tight pocket and extracted the jewelry. Cross pulled the inside handle of the open French door shut as Rick reached out his hand for the outside lever. Cross looped the necklace's leather band between the two interior rotating handles as the first French door aligned with its partner. Rick pulled hard on the door's exterior levers just as Cross finished looping the band between the two levers inside the room. The sudden force of Rick's swing tore the stone dragon off the necklace. The jade pendant remained in Cross's hand as the leather strap strained against Rick's attempted advance. Cross stepped back as Rick pulled again, harder this time. The leather held, stretched to its limit.

The commotion had drawn the attention of the NoviX secretary. She saw Fortinbras' body limp on the floor for the first time and screamed.

The receptionist's muffled cry was doused by an even louder reverberation sound emanating from inside the collaboration room. The echo of an impact filled the glass aquarium like a shark's snout slamming the wall of its confinement to test its strength. The scattering noise of casters followed as the wheeled furniture came to rest on the floor. Alyne had thrown a conference room chair at the exterior window. It ricocheted against the white wall beyond where Fortinbras lay. The unconscious EV3 CTO remained prone, undisturbed by the twang of the vibrating glass. Cross flashed her an approving glance. Her failed attempt gave him an idea. Cross raced to the outside window and positioned himself within reach of the center of the pane.

Rick put more weight into his pull at the opposite side of the room. The Solcom CTO was irate at the barrier between him and his prey. He was crazed, cursing in Mandarin. All of the disappointments of his day, he was directing at Cross and Alyne.

A coral-colored convertible appeared along the building's side roadway between the river and their aquarium wall. The horns on the hood were unmistakable. Jay was piloting his Caddy to dock by the window like a boat arriving at a pier. The vessel stopped a car's width from the window as the necklace band yielded to the force of Rick's pull. Rick fell back on his ass as the French doors flew open but quickly stood to advance into the collaboration room.

Ethan felt the weight of the Maori jade dragon pendant in his palm. He fingered the point of the jewel and positioned it outward away from his skin. With a cupped hand and a fluid rotation of his arm, he slammed the stone against the glass barrier. In one instant, the glass splintered into a spider web. In the next instant, it rained down like a cascade of ice sliding from a frozen roof. Cross had stepped back, unharmed. He grabbed Alyne's wrist with his free left hand, and they jumped the low sill, now covered with broken glass. They took a few well-placed strides toward the Caddy, hurled themselves over the door and into the back seat. Ethan stood to look back, one knee on the leather to stabilize himself as Jay peeled out, readying the vehicle for a quick right toward the front of the building and away to safety.

Rick reached the hole in the building's exterior and leaped adeptly onto the jagged sill. He stood on the shattered glass and raised a fist at the fleeting automobile. Ethan wound back his right arm like a baseball pitcher. He dropped his arm like a trebuchet, hurling the heavy jade stone at Rick. The fastball struck Rick square on the forehead above his eyes, sending him stumbling back into the NoviX collaboration space.

"Bingo!" cried Alyne as she pulled Ethan down from his stance and kissed him on the cheek. "I thought you said we shouldn't throw stones?" She teased as she lost her balance, falling onto Cross's lap from Jay's aggressive right turn around the shrubbery at the building's front corner. Jay accelerated blindly out of the tight turn.

Bam! The Caddy barreled into a bulky man crossing the parking lot on a trajectory to the main entrance steps. The body rolled over the front grill and across the front right hood. The impact tore the Long Horns clear off the face of the car. Cross looked back to see Dante roll to stop and stumble to his feet. He held the Long Horns over his head like a raging bull as Cain raised two fists in the air from a few paces away, standing on the front steps of NoviX. Jay commanded the rugged American car away from the scene along the river's north shore in the harbor's direction. The back seat passengers settled into their seats.

"Jay," Ethan shouted over the whipping wind, "I'm sorry about your car. The horns broke clean off...."

"Sorry? Are you kidding me?! I'm pretty sure that's what those horns were meant for! And besides, everyone dreams of being a get-away heist driver! That was awesome!"

They all shared a hearty laugh. When the moment passed, Cross turned toward Alyne. The wind teased her hair like a fashion designer chasing the perfect look.

"Pitcairn? Fortinbras mentioned it on the phone. I wonder what EV3 is doing there?"

Alyne responded with a pensive look, "I don't know, Ethan. But if I wanted to hide something from the world, no place is more remote."

Jay called back with his eyes on the road, "Where am I taking you?"

Cross said, "Well, I have a friend docked in harbor with a schooner set to sail for Tahiti." Cross looked at Alyne as he confirmed for Jay, "Tahiti. Sounds like an adventure as good as any."

Cross turned to Alyne, "Sound good to you?"

Alyne smiled and squeezed his hand. "I'm in."

| Chapter 17 |

Here There be Dragons

The Ghost Ship was moored south of the airport across the river's mouth at the Port of Brisbane, the city's industrial shipping dock. Dodge had docked away from tourist areas in an attempt to remain discrete. It seemed to Cross that the stealthy swath would stand out like an alien spacecraft parked at a playground wherever it was berthed. Their angular chariot waited among the shipping containers and loading cranes at the edge of Brisbane Harbor. Alyne held Ethan's hand as they made their way down the pier to board the waiting ship. Alyne started their first conversation alone since parting ways with Jay.

"EV3's ARCELOR is a fusion reactor!? That's bloody heavy news, Ethan. And it's portable? Never have I heard of such a Thingummy-bob. That's scarce as rocking horseshit! I understand now why you couldn't tell me and why that hoon Cain wants to keep it secret."

Cross nodded and started to respond as something in front of them caught his attention. "I really can't talk about the ARCELOR. It's...."

Ahead, between the detectives and their unusual transport, a bald man stepped into their path from the shadows between the shipping containers. Sunglasses blocked the Polynesian's eyes from the gaze of Cross and Alyne. A black strap hung from his shoulder, and the man's body blocked their sight of whatever was hanging from it. He held it behind his back with his right arm behind his torso.

Cross released his hand from Alyne's grasp. He sprung his arm in front of her, instinctually protecting her from the danger ahead.

Cross turned his head to whisper to Alyne, keeping his eyes trained on Chan's assistant. "He's got a gun."

Slowly, the Polynesian man ran his right hand's thumb under the shoulder strap to lift the object's weight off his arm. On the wrist of his hand, the image of the head of a dragon came clearly into view. He swung the strap around -holding his arm out toward the sleuths- the object firmly in the clutch of his fist.

An orange handle came into view. "Your backpack," Alyne said. She turned to Cross with a jab, "Really? a gun?"

Cross put his palms up in response as the silent bald man spoke for the first time. He held the bag out to return it.

"It is possible, Mr. Cross, that mankind is on the threshold of a golden age, but if so, it will be necessary first to slay the dragon that guards the door." He held the backpack out to return it to Cross. "I deeply apologize for acting on the will of my former employer. It is not the Maori way. Your pack, sir." The man presented the knapsack.

Cross approached cautiously. "I don't understand. You're not with Rick Chan any longer?" Cross reached out for his small pack.

"We parted ways when he left you in the sea. I implored him to return for you."

"Well, that little maneuver of Chan's help us to solve the mystery," Cross told the man as he donned his backpack. "We discovered Chan's secret undersea receiver panels, and we surmised he's illegally exporting them, which explains why he wanted to keep them under wraps."

The once silent stranger offered more. "Chan's deal to purchase Novix and their technology was set to be the first domino in converting his LEO satellite constellation into an unmatched citizen surveillance network for the Chinese Government. A Chinese-controlled worldwide eye in the sky with data download nodes under the sea in locations all over the planet. I'm afraid there was far more at stake than a company circumnavigating technology export law."

"It's a wicked world, and when a clever man turns his brain to crime, it is the worst of all." Alyne quoted Sherlock Holmes. Cross nodded approval to her well-placed remark.

Ethan wondered aloud, "Chan said his service would focus on the people of rural mainland China. I guess his comment was a literal Freudian slip." Cross pivoted his remarks, "Strange, though, that you view Chan's dealings as bad, but choose to side with Cain and EV3."

"Strange indeed." Alyne echoed. "Chan lost his bid to purchase NoviX to an organization that wants to use the nano-tech solar panels as a diversion to other clandestine technology."

"It is a mistake to confound strangeness with mystery." The Maori man suggested, "The mystery was never Solcom and their use of NoviX nanotechnology. The mystery is to discover what Cain is doing on Pitcairn and ask why?"

"So, you traded one bad boss for another bad guy. Cain should not be trusted." Again Cross wondered what evil plan Cain was hatching on the island.

The Polynesian with the dragon underlined by illegible script tattooed to his wrist offered a perspective that had only briefly crossed Ethan's mind. "Cain may not be bad. You must view the world as he does. See what could be and ask, why not?" *Cain, not a bad guy?* The thought was difficult for Ethan to swallow.

"Naw, Yeah, it still seems shady. EV3 wants NoviX technology to shield whatever they are doing with their ARCELOR on Pitcairn?" Alyne asked Cross and the once silent stranger.

Pitcairn. It was the place that Fortinbras had uttered. It was the island that Doctor Dodge had told them about on the sail back to Brisbane. It was the location Dodge had been trying to reach via HAM for years, the place that had gone silent key. "What do you know about EV3's dealings on Pitcairn?" Cross asked the bald man.

"A little knowledge is a dangerous thing. I know only that Cain has interests there. I am cautious to theorize. Insensibly one begins to twist facts to suit theories, instead of theories to suit facts." The bald man quoted Holmes. Alyne nodded with respect, impressed.

Cross pondered the enigmatic statement. "What are the chances of us encountering Cain at NoviX?" Cross asked a rhetorical question that permeated his thoughts.

"Same as the chances of you being sent to Rocket Sci after meeting me in Dubai days earlier, I'd say." Alyne offered evidence of another chance encounter. It seemed her mind was hard at work trying to make sense of their entanglement too.

"Or the chances that Chan knew to send you to find us in Bondi?" Cross directed his comment at the Polynesian. Alyne looked equally perplexed.

"I don't believe in chance." said the man. "There are only encounters in history. The world is full of obvious things which nobody by any chance ever observes." more

Holmes, thought Cross. The man turned to Cross, "From your first phone call in Dubai, I knew where the evidence might lead you." Cross remembered the man had stood near him at the indoor ski area when Logan had first called him about the enigmatic rocket fairings and realized he had overheard the conversation in its entirety. "Life is infinitely stranger than anything which the mind of man could invent."

"Indeed," offered Cross realizing now that chance may have played little part in the escapade. "Thank you for returning my effects. Shall we be concerned about EV3's activity on Pitcairn?"

"Every positive value has its price in negative terms... the genius of Einstein leads to Hiroshima. If you have the means, it seems Cain's dealings on Pitcairn should be checked." He pointed to a Latin anagram tattooed in fine scripted text under the dragon on his arm. The palindromic text read the same forward and back,

"In girum imus nocte et consumimur igni"

The islander translated its meaning to English, "We go in a circle at night and are consumed by fire." The man finished the exchange with the same Maori farewell that Cross had first heard Beck Peters use in New Zealand, "Kia ora, I must be on my way back to Hawaiki." The Maori man passed between Cross and Alyne, toward Brisbane and the setting sun. The pair of gumshoes turned their heads together to follow the enigmatic figure.

The sun dipped below the western edge of Australia as the pair turned back east. Dodge appeared ahead of them at the top of the Ghost Ship's lowered rear gate. Interior lights framed his silhouette, making him look like an apparition. He said, "What are you two waiting for? You look like you've seen a Ghost." Dr. Dodge joked about his Schooner, but the comment seemed après peau. "You two ready to finish the work the Sea Gull started? An exploration expedition into the South Pacific? To Tahiti!" he shouted with enthusiasm. He extended his hand, "Shall we?" They boarded the craft in the shadow of the sun and set a course across Moreton Bay into the Coral Sea, forever after eve.

| Epilogue |

Project Palindrome

Cross took a seat at the side of his supervisor inside the Secret Compartmentalized Information Facility conference room. Just over a dozen other people filed into the windowless space of the secure access area at Cross' employer. It had been a long time since he had participated in a Top Secret level briefing that was so well attended. Usually, only classified design reviews had a room full of participants. He made his way into the largest classified SCIF Cross' company had. It was filling up fast with visitors in dark suits. People Cross didn't recognize. Besides a young security officer with brown hair that Cross didn't know, no coworkers joined Cross and Logan. Everyone else was from out of town, and no one was smiling. All that Logan had shared with Cross prior was that the meeting was an out brief of an investigation that had commenced nearly a year ago, an investigation triggered by the report on EV3 and the ARCELOR that Cross had filed upon his return from London. Logan's young security officer secured the SCIF entrance. She set the classification level and offered the obligatory escape route instructions for an emergency.

"Can I have your attention for a moment?" the graceful officer stated, standing by the only door to the room as the group settled into chairs around the long conference room table. The crowded room was stifling.

"You are all here for an indoctrination and status report on the Palindrome Project. Today's briefing will be at the Top Secret SCI level. Caveat Palindrome. In the unlikely event of a fire, you will exit through this door, to the left and out of the SCIF. Follow the main hallway the same way you entered. The EXIT signs will guide you to the main lobby." The small-framed woman gestured with her arms like an airline attendant as she provided the instructions. Cross smirked, imagining the officer continuing with, *"In the unlikely event of a water landing, your seat cushion will double as a floatation device."* The room was cramped with unfamiliar people. Cross wished oxygen masks would drop from the ceiling tiles as the brunette continued. "I'll turn it over now to Mr. Blaise and our guests from the Central Intelligence Agency who traveled up from Langley last night to provide this briefing."

A large glass board flickered to life at the end of the room, projecting the CIA emblem. A muscular black man rose from the table as he advanced the image on the screen with some unseen remote. It changed to a giant world map centered on the Pacific Ocean. The continents were outlined by a subtle blue glow that made them appear to hover over the seas. Cross glanced down at his wristwatch, recognizing the familiar, rare view of the globe. It was 9 am.

"Good morning. I am Dewane." Cross smiled to himself again. It was common for personnel in the intelligence community to use only their first name. It was a habit born from careers steeped in concern for operational security. In a setting like this, thought Cross, in a room within a room within a secure facility, it was an extreme behavior. Cross guessed that Dewane had even signed the SCIF visitor log using his first name only and as SELF under the Organization. Cross found it ironic, considering Dewane's briefing started with a giant CIA logo. Everyone here knew from where the speaker hailed, and Cross' security coworker had introduced Blaise using his surname. Dewane wasn't fooling anyone within the room by omitting his last name and his title. Instead, Cross just found himself confused about the man's rank and relative importance in the organization. Or maybe that was the point. At any rate, it was a passing thought; Cross didn't care much about that sort of organizational status. To him, it was just extraneous information.

The sharply dressed speaker commanded attentiveness from the audience. He seemed to hold a position of prominence. The man wore his authority as snugly as his finely tailored suit, but Cross sensed the man was suppressing a jovial personality for this serious professional occasion. He continued. "We are providing you the same briefing we provided to the Sec Dev at the Pentagon last week. Each of your organizations will play a prominent role in Project Palindrome. Please consider this a kick-off of sorts for the new program." He advanced the image on the glass board with a hand gesture. Hundreds of blue dots appeared on top of the map. It seemed that there was a point of light in nearly every country. Clusters of blue dots could be seen in the more industrialized areas of the world. "What you're looking at here are all the companies known to do business with EV3."

EV3. Cross was aware of EV3's small empire. His report was the first to have correlated the ARCELOR technology to the company's cruise line subsidiary, PANACEA. Cross knew EV3 was also involved with the biomedical industry, and of course, he was familiar with its military dealings due to his exposure to the CENTURI program and the ARCELOR. Still, he was surprised to see such an extensive footprint.

"EV3," Dewane continued, "seems to operate under various names and alias. The most recent organizational title is registered in Great Britain is Energy Ventures and Electronics Enterprises. It is operated by a baron CEO named Nathan Cain, who owns and operates many other associated subsidiary companies such as PANACEA, a global cruise line. He has recently acquired NoviX, a developer of advanced solar panels constructed from carbon nanotubes." Kraft glanced at Cross, and Cross sent back a silent nod. Indeed, they knew more about that merger than anyone in the room. "The most significant evidence of the extent of Ev3's influence, and perhaps the most concerning, is their involvement with the International Thermonuclear Experimental Reactor, ITER. Mr. Cross, here, submitted a report that suggests EV3 has had a hand in delaying the progress of that multinational-funded project to maintain their market lead with the ARCELOR, albeit, secret market lead. To do so, EV3 seems to have infiltrated both the International Atomic Energy Agency and Euratom. The level of political manipulation required for this feat is staggering. We are dealing with a powerful organization here." The stakeholders in the room seemed aware of this severe and compromising indictment. No one reacted as Dewane continued. "The dots in blue represent entities that trade with EV3 and its subsidiaries, both customers and suppliers."

The stately man advanced the image again. The map remained as more than half of the blue dots morphed to red dots. "This is a view of the companies known to supply EV3's various operations. The agency has traced the global money movement to confirm that EV3 has issued payment for a good or service to each of the entities highlighted in red within the preceding year." Logan's expression changed. His hand rose to rub his beard in a subtle attempt to cover his mouth. Cross couldn't place the reaction. Surprise? Shame? Guilt? *Odd.*

Cross turned his attention back to Dewane. He had heard that the CIA was predominantly staffed by economists. Contrary to the pop culture persona that the CIA mainly employed James Bond-like secret agent characters, the Agency recruited the top analysts from the finance world to monitor monetary exchanges, a leading indicator of activity of any sort, nefarious or otherwise. Dewane took a deep breath and walked to the other side of the glass board screen.

"We have observed an uptick in billing activity in recent months. We believe this to be an indication of payments for deliveries. Our analysts are hard at work to generate a composite view of what EV3 may be building based on the types of businesses concerned. The task is proving to be a challenge due to the disparate nature of the companies involved. Every organization in red is an accomplice until our analysts prove them innocent. All are considered participants, knowingly or unknowingly enabling EV3 and will be subject to asset seizure, financial suspension, or worse." Cross considered that for a moment. He imagined a room somewhere full of analysts highly educated in finance trying to draw conclusions about EV3's intentions and technical pursuits from a box of parts emptied on a table. The scene felt like a jury attempting to deliberate on a murder verdict before a trial. They could conclude almost anything from the evidence laid out before them. He hoped the Agency employed an engineer or two to help fit the puzzle pieces together with some context.

"Another thing we have observed is an increase in shipments to a single location." Dewane advanced the image to reveal an overlay of a series of shipping routes crisscrossing the world's oceans. Most of them converged on a point of light now boldly illuminated among the others. It was located in the South Pacific, thousands of miles from the nearest continent. Dewane pointed with a meaty finger. "The Island of Pitcairn," Dewane paused for emphasis. "This isolated spot in the South Pacific, more than 3,000 miles from any continent, receives supplies weekly. The closest inhabited territory is the equally remote Easter Island over 1,100 miles to its east. It appears that nearly every PANACEA cruise line passing through the South Pacific en route to New Zealand or Australia or returning to England via Cape Horn passage makes a stop there, at Pitcairn. Each ship is greeted by a smaller tender boat that departs from the main island.

And what's more, Pitcairn is not an excursion stop. PANACEA literature only offers Fiji and Tahiti as destinations available to passengers on those routes, but Pitcairn is not mentioned in their brochures." Curious, thought Cross as the sentiment was shared around the room. He thought of the PANACEA vessels he had seen in Sydney harbor and from the shore of Tahiti last month before he and Alyne had to part ways with Dr. Dodge and with each other. Theirs would be another relationship to fall victim to geographical separation, just like he and Ila. He took solace from the words he remembered from Ila's horoscope: *Something ends in order for something else to start anew.* Cross thought, one day, maybe his job's relentless travel cadence would subside enough for him to get to know a local girl. He pushed the thought of Alyne aside, choosing to focus instead on the revelation that EV3 was using their extensive cruise line operations for dual purposes, passenger and freight delivery. But what freight?

"Our satellite imagery has revealed a significant build-up of facilities." Dewane advanced the charts again, showing a high-resolution image of the remote island. The evidence of active construction was all over the isolated patch of land. Dewane pointed to a couple of locations on the island map. "Significant facilities we can see in this image include large smokestacks, and this here may be evidence of a small rocket launch complex. These large storage tanks are believed to be part of a water desalination facility." Dewane walked back to the other side of the screen.

"We know that the British Government sold or leased this tiny territory to a corporation just over a decade ago. The remaining locals were relocated, and the business began to set up shop almost immediately after that. That corporation was EV3. It is unclear what they are building, but they have taken measures to protect it. The 500-foot cliffs nearly all around the island make it naturally well fortified; We have evidence that a network of undersea microphones has been installed to warn of approaching underwater activity. We know that a commercial 360-degree radar system is installed on this tower," Dewane pointed to a structure on a hill, "presumably to monitor approaching air and sea activity around the island. However, it's strange that we've recorded no other radio signals despite a few test transmissions after the installation was complete. From a SIGINT standpoint, the island has been radio silent for many years."

As Cross squinted his eyes to study the image, a voice at the table asked the question that was on everyone's mind. Cross kept his eyes trained on the picture of Pitcairn as he listened, "What does the CIA think EV3 is doing at Pitcairn?"

Dewane cleared his throat. "Whatever they are doing, they are keen to keep it secret. In light of the recent intelligence provided by Logan Kraft's organization and based on the observations reported by Mr. Cross of EV3 operations and their ARCELOR," Dewane paused again for emphasis, "We believe Cain's operation on Pitcairn is in support of the development of a pure fusion bomb. Our analysts postulate that an ARCELOR-based weapon would have none of the radiation fallout associated with a traditional fission-triggered hydrogen fusion bomb like the ones in the US arsenal today. The military advantage that such a power can afford an adversary is obvious. Enemy forces could advance on the targeted area shortly after impact without risk of radiation harm to their own forces."

What!? The statement broke Cross' concentration. He turned from the map and stared at Logan in disbelief. Logan's surprised expression indicated it was the first time he'd heard of the theory as well. It didn't make sense. Cross' report had presented facts and did nothing to suggest that EV3 was developing a bomb. There was literally no evidence that would lead to a conclusion of this sort. It was correlation without causation. A fusion reactor was an entirely different device than a fusion bomb. The only thing they had in common was the word fusion. Cross was astonished and spoke.

"What evidence do you have that EV3 is developing a fusion bomb?!" The supposition seemed so fantastic. Only the gravity of the indictment suppressed Cross' laughter.

"Our analysts have based their conclusion on your report of the ARCELOR fusion device, Mr. Cross. It's all in the Palindrome indoc package we've provided to Logan, along with the few encrypted communications we intercepted and have yet to decode. We have no time to waste. Project Palindrome is our last opportunity for intelligence before we strike." *A little knowledge is a dangerous thing*, Cross reflected.

Their theory was sophomoric! Had they been watching too many action films? Analysts? How could they call themselves analysts? Did they just run with the most obvious idea from their first conversation around the water cooler? If ever there was an example of twisting facts to suit theories instead of theories to suit facts, this was it. Cross didn't take long to play out the dire consequences of the backward tactic that the CIA proposed: fire, aim, ready. This conclusion was the last thing Cross thought anyone would draw from the information in his report or any of the evidence in hand, for that matter. Cross's frenzied gaze met Logan's. Logan put his hand on Cross' shoulder to suppress his reaction. Dewane continued.

"At this classification caveat, you can know that the Palindrome Project is our attempt to gain boots on the ground intel at Pitcairn. We want to get personnel onto that island." Dewane advanced the charts to zoom out once again. The Pacific-centered map had returned this time clear of shipping routes and dots. Pitcairn remained highlighted in what now seemed like an eerie blue glow. "We can't approach by boat or submarine. Infiltrating cargo delivered by ship is hampered by the long transit time and the tender exchange. Not to mention, we aren't clear on what is being delivered. Our best chance at getting near the island is by aircraft." But didn't Dewane already mention there was radar on the island? What were they going to propose next? A G.I. Joe halo jump from a stealth plane? Cross was ready to be entertained by another ill-conceived notion.

"We don't want to provoke a military response by approaching with a military, marine asset." Ok, thought Cross, there is a glimmer of adult supervision within an adolescent plan. "There is no runway on the island and nowhere else close to land, so an aircraft that can remain aloft for an extended period is needed to launch a mission from the nearest land thousands of miles away and return." Cross thought that many aircraft might be capable of that. He wondered if Dewane was about to propose the Intellagama? Its long-range endurance and water landing ability would suit the task well. "We evaluated several commercial options and have settled on a solution proposed by Mr. Cross' report." This should be good, thought Cross. What was the next hair-brained conclusion they made from his write-up? "The CENTURI."

What!? The CENTURI was military. Even the most benign configuration for police surveillance and crowd control wouldn't be viewed as a civilian or commercial aircraft. Did they think someone monitoring the Pitcairn radar terminal would say, it's ok, it's only a civilian drone approaching? Maybe they have mail for us? Besides, the CENTURI didn't carry people. It was an Unmanned Aerial Vehicle. *Unmanned!*

Dewane continued with a proud grin as he advanced

the slide to show a cutaway of the flying saucer-shaped vehicle. A top-down cross-sectional view of the craft's 10-meter diameter filled the screen. "With intel from Mr. Cross' report, we are proposing to retrofit the ARCELORs in a small group of CENTURI's with the new firmware alteration to the power supply advised by Cross that will allow the crafts to fly for weeks." Dewane smiled grimly. "We're using their precious ARCELOR technology against them. Someone in our office thought it to have a little poetic justice. Project Palindrome. What goes around comes around, like a boomerang."

For real!? Thought Cross. Wasn't there a less complex concept? How would a CENTURI deliver a person to the island? What about that radar? As if reading Cross' thoughts, Dewane continued.

"EV3 operates a radar on the island intermittently, and the CENTURI's aren't stealth. However, they have a naturally low Radar Cross Section, not much more of an RCS than a crow or a raven, so we have also generated a specification for Logan and his team to alter the standard six CENTRI triangle formations. We are proposing a V-shaped formation with flight characteristics that mimic the natural behavior of migrating birds. We'll have the approaching CENTURIs follow a common seasonal migratory pattern as they pass nearby on a trajectory to Antarctica. These enhancements to the CENTURI fall squarely in the wheelhouse of Logan's organization, which is why we've gathered here today. What do you say, Logan? Are these feasible modifications to the CENTURI flight controls? How long will it take to implement these changes?"

Logan sat up. Cross leaned in, biting his tongue, waiting for the VP to speak first. Cross was annoyed. Migrating birds!? That was his idea. He was confident the changes could be made to make the formation appear more natural in short order. It might take him a day or two to alter and test the code. Logan Responded.

"We'll need a least a few months," Logan stated as he sensed Cross wanting to speak up. He turned his head ever so slightly toward Cross' as a nonverbal gesture to Cross to put his objection in check. Cross got the signal and sat back, still astonished by the ill-informed conclusions.

Dewane looked to a grey-haired man seated at the table. The man responded to Dewane,
"That's still before the solar eclipse."
"Good," said Dewane.
What did the timing of the upcoming solar eclipse have to do with the CIA's plan? Cross thought.
Dewane spoke again, this time to Logan, "Mr. Kraft, if you'll kindly excuse yourself along with Mr. Cross, I'd like to discuss another aspect of the project with the other stakeholders. I'm afraid it's a caveat level for which you will not be granted a need-to-know."

Logan nodded in acknowledgment. Cross sensed his mentor might be harboring some annoyance of his own, but he was doing well to hide it. He exited with professional crispness, signaling to Cross and the young security officer to join him as he stood and moved toward the exit.

Cross grabbed his mentor's arm after the door had shut outside the room, stopping him in the SCIF hallway where they could still speak openly about classified information.

"Logan, I'm not convinced they've reached the right conclusion in there. I'm no fan of Cain, but building a bomb on Pitcairn? It doesn't sound like him. They are proceeding as though a set of facts are true such that they can conveniently marshal a specific political agenda." The statement stopped the brunette from walking a pace ahead of them. She turned to listen. Kraft spoke with the authoritative voice of a VP/GM.

"I share your frustration Cross, but it's not our role to influence policy or to do any more than advise on tactics, techniques, or procedures for the equipment we sell. It's the government's job to implement policy. We just provide tools." Logan answered with finality, but there was worry in his eyes. "There's something more concerning for us, Ethan." Logan peered at the security officer, pulling her into the conversation as he turned back to Cross, "Our organization is one of those red dots. We are supplying EV3 with hardware, and I know what it is." Logan paused for emphasis. "Hopefully, I bought us a few months in there to figure out what EV3 is using it for before the CIA discovers there is more that we provide to EV3 than parts and services for the CENTURI."

"What is it?" Both the security officer and Cross

asked the question in unison. They smiled briefly at each other, amused at their shared response.

"Follow me to my office. I'll show you."

| Mark of Cain |

Hiddenite is the Trace Element.
What is the Silent Key?

X G K H D Y Z

P V D C K L X C F N I T Z G P A H A E L T A M B Z V Q O J P N H Y M N T P M G M H M B B Q D W W I K L K F U A A P

W G A P Y R T N E P H M L Y O P U M M K A E I F S W F A T U L Z A C B J M B N P N M Y V Z L H T Q H U

E M Y L M V G I G C P T L W L V C F P A A W W B U Y Z P K L K A L T C F S Q F U B Z B B Q V M J

N B U L Y F S I Y K K V A M F L S P P B T N L A X B S M L O I X A H Q Y B H A P Y X T O S B

H U M M F L Z N I G N Q P Q W Q Q M T U L U Z Z B S M K J I H F L S P Q M

A P Y M C K P T H Y E C X W A L D X O C G M Y Q E G Y V Z Y H P Z L N M L Z Y H P

W X M Z H

| About the Author |

R. W. Bell has spent nearly two decades steeped in the impenetrable world of the defense industry. He has led development efforts on covert projects ranging from the fabled US Army Comanche Stealth Helicopter to cutting-edge aircraft survivability equipment for the Ministry of Defense. He holds a Top Secret clearance and three advanced degrees in aerospace engineering. He is a helicopter pilot and operates drones for the US government. His work on electronic warfare systems and countermeasures has sent him across the globe to dozens of countries and undisclosed locations. R. W. Bell never expected he'd write a book, until he had to.

Uncover more at https://rwbellnovels.com

| **Ever After Eve** |
for my daughter

Start each day with laughter
Everyday's an eve
An eve before ever after
A day before you leave

For someplace new
For somewhere grand
A special time to come
Everyday's an eve, you know,
Don't waste a single one

Today's the eve that you prepared
For something great ahead
Your careful plans
Your patient plots
May all washout, instead...

Plan for rain and overcast
And happy you will be
When fog gives way
To the sunny day
That you set out to see

Weigh your anchor
Cast a line
Horizon bound you are
Today's the eve that you set sail
for the brightest shining star

Let your smile guide the way
Tomorrow is an eve
The grin that started yesterday
May meet a frown, believe

You'll find your way around with laughter
This ever after eve

www.ingramcontent.com/pod-product-compliance
Lightning Source LLC
Chambersburg PA
CBHW072349110726
47909CB00003B/654